RIDE LIKE THE WIND

Cowgirls in Time Romance Series

A Chill Wind

Wind Beneath My Wings

Against the Wind

The Healing Wind

Ride Like the Wind

RIDE LIKE THE WIND

Erica Einhorn

Ralston Store Publishing
P.O. Box 1684
Prescott, Arizona 86302

ISBN 978-1-938322-28-0

Professionally and lovingly edited by:
Jennifer Hope
www.MesaVerdeMediaServices.com

Printed in the USA.

Dedicated to the one I love . . .

CHAPTER ONE

WHEN MARY ELIZABETH stepped out the door, she saw that the horse and wagon waited for her by the side of the barn. She smiled and was grateful that her father, John Mills, had hitched up the horse before he left. His job—president of the local bank—was more than a job to him, it was his life. And although he preferred taking the wagon to work, when Mary Elizabeth had to go into town to buy supplies, he was willing to ride his horse. He had gotten up extra early to get the wagon ready for her. She was lucky to have a father like that, and she knew it, though she wished that he'd extend that kindness in other areas, as well.

Mary Elizabeth stroked the horse, climbed into the wagon, and asked Old Cookie to move forward. Cookie was the horse she learned to ride on. And when she was a girl, she loved to ride like the wind, her long blonde hair flying behind her and Cookie barely needing any encouragement. Then, as Mary Elizabeth grew older, she lost interest in riding, though she couldn't remember what took its place. Certainly not the cooking and cleaning and chores that she learned to do around the house.

Old Cookie and the wagon moved down the wide tree-lined street. She liked how the trees would blot out the sky unless you drove down the center of the street where the branches didn't go. But this time of year, the branches were all bare. The thought made her shiver. Her family had moved to Red Bluff, Colorado, from Atlanta, Georgia. John Mills had been a banker there, and her family lived in town. When the Civil War broke out, John Mills, who was an abolitionist while all his neighbors were farmers who owned slaves, had become an outcast. Somehow the family made it through and past those dark years, but it was never the same. Her brother had been beaten up many times over the conflict. He had eventually left town and moved north to Des Moines, Iowa. But John Mills didn't move the rest of his family west until a year ago.

At first, they stayed at the local hotel with Eliza and Samuel McKenna, the lovely people who owned the hotel. When the Mills house was finally completed—a wonderful little two bedroom at the far end of town— they had moved into that. It had enough room out back for a small barn for the horses, a corral, a large garden, and a chicken house where the chickens, allowed to run free during the day, were closed up at night. Although the Mills family lived in town, the foxes and other wild animals were close enough to kill or maim the chickens. When they first moved into this house, a fox had come in and killed five chickens in one night. They thought they had moved into a civilized place and were all surprised at the carnage the fox had left behind.

When they first discussed plans for the house, they talked of having just one bedroom for themselves and a loft for Mary Elizabeth to sleep in. If she had been younger, that is the way it would have turned out. But at twenty-five years old, any hopes of marriage were long past, so they had decided on two bedrooms. It wouldn't be long now that people would be referring to her as the old spinster.

Mary Elizabeth sighed and shook her head. There was a time when Sheriff Josiah had asked her to have supper with him. She had turned him down, of course. She would rather be alone as she is, living in her parents' house, than living somewhere alone as a widow. Besides, he was already in love with Jenna, the woman he eventually married. Although she didn't know that then, still she didn't want to be courted by a sheriff. There was more chance of him dying than living.

And when the schoolmarm, Annie, had married Henry Ralston, the former storekeeper, and moved out of town, Mary Elizabeth's mother had wanted her to apply for the job. Reluctantly, she did, more for her mother than for herself. No, that was wrong—*completely* for her mother. So she was secretly glad when another woman, Rachel, was hired. She had appeared almost out of thin air, although Mary Elizabeth had seen her around town a time or two before. It was almost as if all of them had appeared out of thin air: Jenna, her friend Sarah, Granny, Rachel, and Jenna's brother Ryan. And Jenna and Ryan's other sister, Kat, had recently moved to town and married the doctor. Then there was Nick who was now the new deputy sheriff.

But looking at it objectively, and Mary Elizabeth liked to look at everything objectively, one could say that her family had appeared out of thin air, also. They had *suddenly* appeared here after more than a thousand-mile trip from Atlanta. But when *her* family had arrived, they were worn out and bedraggled from the trip. Jenna and her lot looked as if they had come over from the next town, and that is not where they had come from. Few people knew exactly where they had come from, and those who did know weren't talking.

There was that birthday party at the hotel—for Granny's birthday. The whole town was invited, and Mary Elizabeth attended only because she was living in the hotel at the time. But there were these incredibly delectable desserts that she had never seen or tasted before. Everyone in town thought they were amazing, but Jenna, Ryan, Granny, Kat, Nick, and Rachel all took them for granted. Where do things like that come from? Certainly not from anywhere around here. And she had never seen anything like that even in Atlanta.

Thinking back on that party, she smiled. She had talked to Ryan there. Ryan Leyton, who was Jenna and Kat's brother, and who now owned Ralston General Store. He had bought it when Henry Ralston left town. That was a blessing. If you wanted to go shopping while Henry owned the place, you had to devote hours to the endeavor. Henry would not let you leave without talking so much that you wanted to scream before you got out of there. Ryan was quiet. Ryan was creative. Ryan was handsome. They had talked briefly at the party, and she had been madly in love with him ever since.

Of course she knew that was completely stupid. A man like Ryan could have any woman he wanted, and men like that liked fresh eighteen-year-olds. He would never notice a twenty-five-year-old "old maid" like her. He probably just talked to her at the party out of compassion. She had found him very sensitive, especially when he talked of his paintings. Mary Elizabeth had liked that he was a painter—a creative sort—like her. And although she had gone to the store at least once a month since that party, they had never spoken again. Not for lack of trying on her part. But it always seemed that her mother was with her or someone else was in the store either talking to him or searching the store for something they needed. There was never a chance for her to approach him, to even ask how he was doing or what painting he was working on. And when it came time to pay for her purchases, his good looks stunned her so much that all she could do was mumble "thank you" and stumble out the door.

Ryan had curly black hair that looked like he hadn't combed it in a month. But the hair framed his face and made those intense blue eyes even more attractive. But it wasn't just his looks that had charmed her. He had the most genuine gracious manner of being, always polite and soft-spoken, and the way he looked into her eyes when he handed her change— She couldn't sleep for a week afterward thinking back on those eyes boring into hers, exploring their depths, and she knew—she just knew—that he must be very aware of her feelings toward him. And that made her feel exposed and vulnerable, which made her uncomfortable and even less apt to want to talk to him. At the same time, she craved being able to talk to him and to feel those eyes on her.

She didn't even have to pull up on the reins. When Mary Elizabeth pulled the wagon up next to the store, Cookie stopped automatically. She had made enough trips here to know the routine. Mary Elizabeth climbed out of the wagon, took a deep breath, put her hand on the door handle, and prepared herself to be in the company of the most attractive man she had ever met.

CHAPTER TWO

HE HAD LIVED here in the nineteenth century for nearly a year now, ever since his sister Jenna had discovered the cave that led from the twenty-first century back here to the nineteenth. During that time, he had sold his art store in the new Red Bluff, bought the Ralston General Store here, and lived happily ever after. Except for one thing. There weren't many women in this town. That didn't matter, though, because Ryan only had eyes for one. Mary Elizabeth Mills.

Ryan saw her before she entered the store. Even while in deep conversation with the sheriff, Josiah, and his best friend, Nick, who was Josiah's deputy, Ryan knew she was there before the wagon even parked outside the window. He always knew. And when he saw her climb out of the wagon, an inner trembling began, and he completely lost track of the conversation.

"Ryan? Where are you?"

"Huh, what? Oh! What'd I miss?"

The other two men laughed, and Nick whistled under his breath. "She's a beauty all right, Ryan. I could go for her in an instant."

"You can forget that, Nick." Josiah watched her as she walked to the front door. "She wouldn't even have supper with me because she said she didn't want to be a widow. I imagine the risk would be the same with you."

"Stay away from her, Nick. She's mine." He spoke to the men, but his eyes never left Mary Elizabeth.

"Are you dating her?" asked Nick.

"Nick!" Josiah spoke sharply. "Stop being so twenty-first century. You don't date women here. You *court* them."

Nick laughed. "Are you *courting* her, then?"

"Not yet," said Ryan, as Mary Elizabeth walked through the door. "Hallo, Miss Mills."

"Isn't that a little formal?" Nick asked under his breath, and then aloud, "Hallo."

"Howdy, Ma'am," said Josiah.

"Gentlemen," said Mary Elizabeth, with a slight curtsy.

Ryan watched as her eyes briefly met his before she turned to her shopping. He loved her looks. She had the tiniest waist he had ever seen. His sister Jenna had told him it was from a corset, but still, even without, it had to be really small. And he couldn't help but notice her big boobs. He shrugged his shoulders. He was a boob man. What could he say? And the way she walked and presented herself, elegant, like she was a queen or something. Some would call that arrogant, but whatever it was, he liked it.

"Ryan!" Nick stamped his foot to get his attention.

"What? Oh, yeah, sorry."

"When did Samuel and Eliza leave to find their son?" Nick spoke louder than necessary to get his attention.

"I drove them to the next town, you know, Pink

Springs, a few days ago." Ryan tried to keep his gaze and his concentration on Nick and the conversation, but they both drifted to Mary Elizabeth. They always did when she was in his store. And for some reason, whenever she was there, so many other people were around that he couldn't even have a conversation with her. They hadn't really had a conversation since Granny's party, and that was nearly a year ago.

"You drove them? What do you mean?" asked Nick.

Josiah answered for him, quietly. "Nick, you're acting twenty-first-century again. He drove them with a horse and wagon, of course."

The three men laughed. Nick had recently moved to the *old* Red Bluff to be the deputy sheriff. Since Jenna had her baby, Josiah wanted to spend more time at home with his family instead of at the sheriff's office all the time. And the previous deputy, Rawlins, had left town some time before. Nick was still trying to get used to how things were in the nineteenth century.

"Yeah, dropped them off. You should have seen how excited they were! They haven't seen him in so many years, and all this time they thought he was dead."

Nick nodded. "They must be excited. Too bad they can't fly," he said casually.

"Nick!" Josiah had been the first one to get involved with someone from the twenty-first century when he married Jenna, Ryan's sister. And he thought that the secret must stay a secret. He didn't want any of the twenty-first-century newcomers to divulge where they actually came from. Josiah thought that was dangerous, so he always reminded people to watch what they said around people who didn't know.

Nick held out his arms. "I meant fly." He moved his

8

arms up and down. "You know, fly, like a bird!" Then he doubled over with laughter as Josiah snorted.

Ryan continued watching Mary Elizabeth who looked like she might almost be finished shopping. He wasn't going to let another day go by without talking to her. "Nick, Josiah," he said under his breath, so only they could hear, "I think it's time you guys go back to your office. Don't you?" Smiling a big smile, he looked at them and nodded toward the door.

"No, we don't have to—" started Nick when Josiah elbowed him. "Oh, yeah, of course. Yeah, we're leaving right now. Bye." He and Josiah walked out, Nick suppressing a giggle.

Ryan hoped that Mary Elizabeth didn't hear the giggle. She looked like she had finished her shopping, although she kept looking at the shelves as she walked slowly up to the money box. Then she was standing before him, placing her items on the counter. When she looked up, he looked into the clearest and brightest brown eyes that he had ever seen. She wore her dark blonde hair in a tight bun, which made her look uptight, but underneath, Ryan could feel her vulnerability. And he liked it.

Ryan picked up the first item, a five pound bag of rice, and wrote down the price. He did the same for the rest: a gallon of molasses, a pound of lard, and a pound of butter. Then he looked up at her—she was a tall woman, nearly as tall as he was. "Is there anything else, Miss Mills?"

"Yes, twenty-five pounds of flour, and twenty-five pounds of sugar, if you don't mind carrying them out to the wagon for me." She nodded toward her wagon, visible out the side window. Before he had a chance to answer, she said, "You took Eliza and Samuel to the stage?"

"Yes, they had found out from—" he hesitated. He couldn't tell her that Jenna had found on the internet that their son was still alive, even though he had been presumed dead all these years. "They had word that their son was still alive, so they went back East to get him."

She nodded. "Oh, that's good. Well, I was wondering if you would consider taking me to the stage this coming Wednesday?" The edges of her mouth turned up into a nervous smile.

"Well, yeah, of course I would! No problem!" With a huge smile plastered across his face, he added the flour and sugar to her total and gave her the slip of paper. She paid him with nine silver dollars. Before he put them in his cash box, he looked at the dates. He had made a habit of doing that since Zack's big windfall. Zack used to work at the saloon until he discovered the twenty-first century and started living with Ryan's niece, Madison. He had discovered a coin worth more than a million dollars. Now, Ryan always checked, and he had bought a coin book for himself—the one that Zack had recommended.

"Is something wrong with the dollars, Ryan?"

Embarrassed, he dropped them into the cash box without looking. "No, no, of course not. Here's your change. Let me get that flour and sugar for you now."

Ryan picked up the flour in one arm and the sugar in the other. Mary Elizabeth grabbed what was on the counter and opened the door for him. After he had secured the two bags into the wagon, he turned and waited to watch her drive away.

"Ryan?"

"Yes, Miss Mills?"

"You are welcome to use this wagon to take me. I'll ride into town with my father. Shall I just stop by on Wednesday when I'm ready?"

"Yes, Miss Mills, that would be perfect. I will be waiting for you."

"Thank you, Ryan." She walked toward the wagon and was just about to step into it, when Ryan hurried over to her and gave her his hand.

When she was safely seated in the wagon, she smiled down at him. "Thank you." Then she urged Old Cookie forward, but before the horse had even taken three steps, she turned around to see Ryan watching her go. "Ryan, you're welcome to call me Mary Elizabeth." Then she smiled and waved, and the horse pulled the wagon down the street. And Ryan could not have been any happier.

CHAPTER THREE

WHEN THE WAGON turned the far corner and was out of
sight of Ryan's store, Mary Elizabeth stole a quick glance
backward. Then she dropped the reins in her lap and
brought both fists up to her head—not hitting herself,
just having a conniption fit. Any other horse may have
speeded up or come to a stop at such loose reins, but Old
Cookie knew what she had to do and where she had to
go, so she kept plodding forward. Mary Elizabeth repeated her parting words in her mind, "You're welcome to
call me Mary Elizabeth!" How could she have said something like that! And smiling down at him like she was
holding court! He must be wondering who I think I am
—Queen Victoria or something! She said aloud in a
mock childish voice, "You are my subject, Ryan, and I
hereby bestow upon you the honor of calling me Mary
Elizabeth!"

"Oh, no! Now I've spoiled everything." She grabbed
the reins and gave a little shake to get Old Cookie to
speed up. Mary Elizabeth wanted to get as far away from
her mistake as fast as possible. The conversation rolled
over in her mind on the way home. And asking him if

there was something wrong with the dollars! What an absurd question! He was just looking at the dates. Big deal. Her father had already told her that the young man, Zack, who had since moved away, had come into the bank on more than one occasion, gone into a room by himself, and looked at the dates on the coins. So although it seemed strange to her, and her father thought it was extremely odd, it wasn't that big of a deal. So she chastised herself for saying anything to him about it.

The only part about the conversation that made her feel good was that she had worked up the courage to ask him to take her to the stage. The idea had never occurred to her before, but when she heard the men discussing that Ryan had taken Eliza and Samuel, then asking him to take her felt like the natural thing to do. Her father may have something to say about it—he had already told her that he would arrange everything—but she'd get around him somehow. After all, she wasn't a little girl anymore who had to do everything that her papa said to do.

That thought made her sad again. No, she wasn't a little girl; she was a twenty-five-year-old woman without a husband. What did her mother keep saying to her? No spring chicken. No, she was no longer a spring chicken, and therefore had little or no chance of anyone asking her to marry. Her father still reminded her, almost daily, of the mistake that she had made not marrying Teddy Thornhill when she had the chance. Teddy Thornhill was dashing and rich and had designs on her. And after her graduation from college when she gave Teddy the mitten, her father had been furious—which she could not understand at all. Her father was a staunch abolitionist. And Teddy's family owned the largest plantation in all of Atlanta—and the largest number of slaves working that plantation. When she asked her father about that, he had said that sometimes you have to overlook certain things. But she not only could not overlook that, she was not in love with him.

Old Cookie started slowing down and made the turn into their driveway. It surprised Mary Elizabeth that they arrived home so quickly, though they didn't live far from town. But her mind had been occupied by going over every aspect of her meeting and conversation with Ryan. Over and over would be more accurate—maybe fifty times in the short trip home. She liked the way he looked at her, but it also made her wonder. Did he look at her like a man who likes the woman he sees, or did he look at her and think, "I better be nice to this poor old spinster, because she'll never find a husband"?

Although she hated feeling like that, she couldn't stop those thoughts from dominating her mind. Of course, it didn't help that her mother made no secret of thinking that Mary Elizabeth was way past her youth and way past the time that any man would want her. Her father still pined away at the loss of Teddy Thornhill. But did *she* really think that it was too late to find a suitable match? The sad truth was that, yes, she did. She had been browbeaten enough by her parents' attitudes, that they had affected her. Now, she, too, thought she was too old. If she was to be completely honest with herself, the truth was that she didn't want a *suitable match*. She wanted love. That's all she wanted. Love. And there was a small part of her that thought it was very important not to give up hope that someday—maybe even soon—she might find the love that she was seeking.

Old Cookie made a wide circle sending the chickens

scattering and then stopped by the side of the barn. Mary Elizabeth climbed out of the wagon, unhitched the horse, and led her into the barn. Then she brushed her out and gave her some grain. Cookie nickered, and Mary Elizabeth stroked her neck. "You're a good horse, Cookie girl. Do you think I'm too old to find a husband, too?" The horse nuzzled her. "Maybe we're both too old then, Cookie, maybe we're both too old."

She grabbed the items she could carry, left the large sacks in the wagon, and walked toward the house. Her thoughts drifted back to Ryan, and with them, a spark of hope. Regardless of what a fool she had made herself out to be with him at the store, she wasn't going to white-wash her feelings. She had set her cap for him, and no one—except maybe Ryan himself—was going to have anything to say about it.

CHAPTER FOUR

RYAN WATCHED THE wagon go slowly down the street, and until it turned he didn't return to the store. Then he skipped into the store, jumped up, and yelled, "Yip Yipee! Yip Yipee!"

"So what's the celebration about, Grandson?" Granny stood at the counter with her arms folded and a big grin on her face. "Let me guess. A woman!"

"Granny! I didn't know you had come in! Good to see you!" He rushed up to her, grabbed her up into his arms, and swung her around and around!

"Ryan! Come on! I'll get sick and barf all over you! Put me down!" Granny struggled to get out of his embrace.

"Oh, sorry, Granny, I got carried away!" Ryan set her back down on the floor.

"I'd say you did. I'd swear that my pacemaker just skipped a beat!" Granny looked at him seriously with her hand on her heart.

"Granny, it did not. What can I get for you? Did you want me to pick up some ice cream next time I go back, um, *there*?" All the people who had moved to the nine-

16

teenth-century Red Bluff from the twenty-first-century Red Bluff, tried not to talk about where or when it was. Too many times someone else had been around whom they hadn't noticed. It just wasn't safe.

"No, Grandson, we don't need any of that sugar. Your sister Kat has informed us that we will be that much healthier if we leave the sugar behind." Kat was his nurse-practitioner sister who had moved to the nineteenth century and married the local doctor, Doc Mercer. She had been a health nut in the twenty-first century, but here, where everything was still natural, she was right in her element.

Ryan shrugged. "What do you need then?"

"Paints. For Edward."

Ryan walked into the back room where he kept his paints and called out, "Which colors does he need?" The paints were only for him and Edward, Granny's husband. No one else in town did any fine-art-type painting. And all the paints were "imported" from the twenty-first century, anyway, so it was just as well.

"How should I know, Grandson? He just said 'paints,' and said that you'd know which ones."

"Granny, this is ridiculous. I have fifty colors back here."

"I don't know what to tell you, Grandson. He said that you'd know."

"Well, do you know what painting he's working on now?" Ryan asked.

"The same one. Since Eliza and Samuel left, there's more work to do."

Ryan dug inside the drawers in his painting cabinet and came up with five tubes of paint. "Eliza and Samuel just left!"

17

Erica Einhorn

"Okay, then, he's just slow!" Granny snorted with laughter.

Ryan walked out and put the tubes of paint on the counter. "These should be the ones that he's looking for: red, orange, yellow, gold, and brown. If he needs anything else, just let me know."

"What do we owe you, Ryan?" Granny scooped up the paints and put them in her bag.

"Same thing you always owe me, Granny: nothing."

"Now how are you going to make a living here if you keep giving everything away?"

Ryan grinned at her. "You know how, Granny. I have a second source of income."

Granny nodded and chuckled. "Yes, we all do at that, don't we?"

After Zack had found that million dollar coin, he had made a list for everyone in town—everyone who came from the twenty-first century, that is. But it had only the highest paying coins on it, which is why Ryan bought his own book. By just going through his coins every day, Ryan had gotten a good second income from coins that were worth five, six, or seven hundred dollars. One time, he did find one worth five thousand, but it was the coins worth a few hundred each that were helping to support him.

"Yes, Granny, we all do. Thanks to Zack!"

"He and Maddie haven't been to town lately. Have you seen them? Do you know how they're doing?"

"Yeah, I see them about once a week. They're having midterms now. They're both doing really well in school."

"Of course, they are. They're bright kids." Granny turned and walked toward the door, and then turned back around.

"Grandson? So who is it, anyway, that you are so excited about? I haven't seen you that excited since you got your first horse!"

Ryan, turning bright red, came out from behind the counter and escorted Granny to the door. "Good-bye, Granny. Nice talking to you!"

"You're not going to tell me, are you? Ryan, I swear, you're acting like a middle schooler with his first crush!"

Ignoring her comment, Ryan opened the door and said, "Let me know if Edward needs any other paints."

Granny stepped out the door and said, "Hmmmph."

Ryan smiled after her, closed the door, and walked back to the counter. He *felt* like a middle schooler with his first crush. Since he had moved back to the nineteenth century, he had been girlfriend-less. And he hadn't been without a girlfriend, since probably middle school. He *always* had a girlfriend—he made sure of that. But since he had moved here, he had been so thrilled to have so much time to paint, that he hadn't given it much thought. Except for Mary Elizabeth, that is. She was often in his thoughts, but it never seemed to work out. And now he would be taking her to the stage, which meant hours together in the wagon. He could hardly wait.

CHAPTER FIVE

IT HAPPENED THE following evening. She knew it would; it had to. There was no way around it. Her father had told her that he would arrange a ride for her to the stage, and she had gone against his wishes and chosen someone for herself.

When her mother set the fried chicken on the table next to the mashed potatoes, her father took the thigh and the leg—he only liked dark meat—nodded to Mary Elizabeth and pointed at her using the chicken leg. "Mr. Smythe's son, Eugene, will take you to the stage."

"Thank you, Papa, but I've already arranged a ride." She said it quietly, hoping he wouldn't hear her clearly enough to react to it. But he heard.

He choked on the bite of chicken he had in his mouth and demanded, "You what?"

"I already arranged a ride for myself. No need to bother Eugene Smythe."

"I told you that I would take care of that for you!" With his fork, he stabbed at the piece of chicken on his plate, missed, and stabbed again.

"I feel more comfortable with Ryan." Mary Elizabeth

20

tried to remain calm, while inside she was longing to run to her room and not deal with this confrontation.

"And who is *Ryan?*" John Mills pounded his fist on the table, and the spoon flew out of the mashed potatoes.

"He owns Ralston General Store."

"That man who bought the store from Henry Ralston? I will not have my daughter traipsing out of town with that no-account!"

"He is not a no-account. He is a very nice man, and I like him." Mary Elizabeth bit her tongue. She should not have confided that bit of information to her father.

"Maybe he isn't a no-account, but he is definitely a mudsill, and I won't have my daughter associating with him."

"Papa, I am twenty-five years old. I will associate with whomever I want." She sounded way more assertive than she felt. She had stood up to him before, but this subject was a touchy one, and she didn't know how far she could—or should—assert herself.

John Mills set down his fork very deliberately and glared at her. "As long as you are living under my roof, you will associate with who *I* tell you to. I'm your father, and I still know what's best for you."

"You know, *Father*," Mary Elizabeth looked him in the eye, "I don't think you do." After putting down her fork, she stood up and walked out of the room.

As she walked, she could see her mother's hand reaching over to her father. "You know, dear, Mary Elizabeth is no spring chicken. She can't be as choosy as she once was." Mary Elizabeth hung outside the door, far enough so that they couldn't see her but close enough to hear the conversation. When her father didn't answer, her mother continued. "I've met this Ryan, and he's a nice enough boy," said Cora Mills.

"He came from *away*!" Her father started eating again; Mary Elizabeth could hear his fork stab at the food on his plate.

"So did we, John, so did we." Her mother patted his hand again and went back to her food.

"But we don't know *where* he came from. *We* came from Atlanta. But no one knows *where* he came from. I don't like it."

"What difference does it make where he comes from, John, as long as she likes him? You don't want your daughter to turn out to be a spinster, do you, John Mills?" Her mother achieved that rare tone of forcefulness that Mary Elizabeth didn't hear very often.

"Hmmmph!" John Mills stabbed at more food on his plate.

Mary Elizabeth, right outside the doorway, suddenly noticed tears falling down her face. It hurt. Being called a spinster, being accused of not being a spring chicken, being talked about as if she were a child. She wanted to sniff, but she didn't dare because they would hear her.

"John, dear, I think you need to go back there, tell her you're sorry, and tell her that Ryan can take her to the stage." Her mother said it slowly, like she was talking to a small child who didn't listen very well.

"Oh, tarnation, Woman! Let me finish my supper first!"

"But Mary Elizabeth is hungry, too, dear," her mother said quietly.

Having had only a few bites of food before walking out, Mary Elizabeth's stomach was complaining, but she didn't feel hungry—didn't think she could eat. The day before she had been happier than she could imagine

22

after Ryan said that he would take her to the stage. And now she felt horrible. She would live with her parents, get old, and die of loneliness. With that thought, she raced to her room, as quietly as she could, threw herself on the bed, and began to cry in earnest. If her father insisted on being such a tyrant, perhaps she should actually consider accepting the job that she was applying for in Farmtown. She didn't want it—she had only applied at her mother's insistence—but maybe getting out from under her father's watchful eye would be the wisest course of action for her. And she enjoyed the city and had even had thoughts that she preferred the city to the sleepy little town where they now lived. It was something that she would have to give some serious thought.

Her parents continued arguing—she couldn't hear the words, just the elevated voices. Then, silence—until she heard footsteps coming down the hallway. She recognized them. It was her mother.

After knocking at the open door, her mother stepped inside, sat beside her on the bed, and patted her back. "Mary Elizabeth," she said and hesitated, "your father just doesn't understand the way women's minds work. And he doesn't understand that when a woman gets older, it limits her choices. I made him see *our* way, and your father has decided to permit you to go with Ryan to the stage."

"Thank you, Mama." Mary Elizabeth sniffed and wiped her eyes, but didn't look up.

"Be sure to get packed tonight, so you can leave with your father first thing in the morning." Her mother patted her on the back again and walked out the door.

Although she was satisfied with the outcome—she would get to go with Ryan—she was furious at her mother's words, and even at the argument her mother had conveyed to her father. Mary Elizabeth hated the whole spring chicken thing and hated being called a spinster. And her choices were limited? She didn't think so. Even if she lived in a large city like Atlanta, she would still prefer Ryan to the other men in town. She wasn't settling for less—she was going after exactly what she wanted: Ryan.

CHAPTER SIX

RYAN THOUGHT BACK on the past year—everything that had happened since he had bought Ralston General Store from Henry. He had done it on a whim. Well, it had looked like a whim to most people, but Ryan had wanted to get out from under the hectic chaos of his art store in the new Red Bluff for quite some time. Suddenly, he had a buyer, and then Henry's store came up for sale, and Ryan bought it and moved, permanently, to the old Red Bluff. About once a week, he made a run to the new Red Bluff to get produce that wasn't available in the current nineteenth century. He had to. There were so many people who had moved from the new Red Bluff who expected salads all year and not just when the garden was ready.

Ryan had done a lot of work during that year— twenty-five paintings started, fifteen of them completed. And he liked them and thought they were good! But whether the public liked them was the true test. Most artists liked their own work, didn't they? And most people who came into the store mentioned how beautiful the paintings were—once he got the nerve to put them up on

25

the walls. But they were just regular people—what did they know about art? Ryan knew what he had to do. He had to work up the nerve to approach a gallery in the new Red Bluff. It's something he had been working toward, but doing it was another thing altogether. What if he failed miserably? The thought made him feel bad.

Then he thought of something else that made his mood brighten: Mary Elizabeth. The following day he would be spending several hours with her. He still couldn't believe it. Over the past year, she had come into the store many times, but there were always other people around keeping him from talking to her. A few times, she came in with her mother, so that didn't work, either. It seemed unbelievable that in all that time, they had never been in the store alone together until the other day.

He remembered one time a few months back when Mary Elizabeth and her mother had walked into the store together. Then her mother left, leaving Mary Elizabeth there without another person in the store. Ryan had just cleared his throat and was getting ready to say something when Nick had come rushing in telling him that he had decided to move here and become Josiah's deputy. Nick was bursting with happiness and carrying a duffle bag full of his clothes, and Ryan didn't have the heart to ask him to leave, even for just a few minutes. So that was one opportunity missed.

Then a month after that, Mary Elizabeth had come in followed by Jenna, Josiah, and their new baby, Milo. By the time Mary Elizabeth had fussed over the baby, her mother had come in and another opportunity was gone. And the difficult part about living in the nineteenth century was that you couldn't just ask for a girl's number and call her up and ask her out. It was done differently here. There were no phones, but there was also a slower pace and a certain way everything was done. There were strict expectations of how girls and boys acted around each other, and Ryan still hadn't figured all of those out. Josiah was right, though. A man did not date a woman here in the nineteenth century; a man courted a woman.

And finally, Ryan would have a chance of setting something up with Mary Elizabeth. He couldn't wait until the following day. Then he wondered what he could possibly set up. Dinner and a movie? Laughing to himself, he shook his head. Obviously no. Movie theaters were a long way off in a future that Mary Elizabeth had no idea of. Eliza had invited Jenna and Josiah over for supper, which had helped them get together. But now Eliza and Samuel were out of town, with Granny and her husband, Edward, taking care of the hotel while they were gone. And not only would Granny not volunteer to cook supper, he couldn't trust the old woman around Mary Elizabeth—at least not until he knew Mary Elizabeth a lot better. Granny was unpredictable and liable to cause him extreme embarrassment that he couldn't live down. No, that was definitely not a possibility. Could he even risk taking Mary Elizabeth to the hotel for supper with Granny and Edward cooking? Even that would be risky. No telling what Granny might say.

And what were his other options? The hotel had the only restaurant in town. And taking her to the new Red Bluff for dinner was not realistic, since Mary Elizabeth had no idea where he—and Jenna, Kat, Granny, Nick, Rachel, and Sarah—had come from. Josiah said that he didn't believe Jenna at first and then when he did, he couldn't accept it. The romance between Jenna and Josiah almost didn't happen because, as Josiah put it, "I

27

was too danged pig-headed to think something like that could work." Now they had a son together. But if Ryan told Mary Elizabeth too soon, he could ruin any chance of a future between them. He would have to play it slow. And he hoped that it would all work out.

CHAPTER SEVEN

HER MOTHER KNOCKED on her door earlier than she had expected. "Mary Elizabeth! Your father is leaving in thirty minutes. If you want breakfast, get up now!"

Mary Elizabeth stepped out of bed and splashed cold water on her face from the bowl on the table. Luckily, she thought, she had finished packing the night before. She quickly dressed and walked down the hallway toward the kitchen. When she heard voices, she instinctively stopped.

"I'll catch a weasel asleep before I allow her to spend time with that mudsill!" Her father had raised his voice, but at least he didn't slam his fist on the table.

"Listen, John," said Cora Mills, "there is a good chance she will get the job, and then you won't have to worry about her association with Ryan. You know that not many women have an education like hers, and if she comports herself well during the interview—and she *will* —then she *will* get the job. You're worrying for nothing. Now stop it and behave yourself. She'll be coming in here any minute."

Mary Elizabeth quietly backed up a few steps, then

stepped loudly on the floor, so they knew she was coming. "Good morning," she said, as she walked into the room.

"Good morning, Mary Elizabeth," said her mother.

"Morning," grumbled her father.

Mary Elizabeth walked to the stove, put the eggs from the pan onto a plate, and sat down. She was not going to let her father get to her—especially not today.

"I'm leaving in ten minutes. If you're not ready, I'm leaving without you." He stuffed the last bite of eggs into his mouth, stood up, and walked from the room.

"Don't worry, dear. He'll be fine. He only wants what's best for you," said her mother, patting her hand.

"What's best for me is what *I* want, not what *he* wants!" Mary Elizabeth stood up, carried her dishes to the bowl on the counter, and poured water over them. In her head, the words, "or what *you* want for me" popped up, although she didn't utter them aloud. But that was where the root of the idea took place. She walked into her room, picked up her suitcase, called, "Good-bye, Mama" over her shoulder, and walked out to wait for her father.

He was climbing into the wagon when he saw her, but he pretended not to. She saw his head jerk around. Didn't he realize how obvious it was? She lifted her suitcase into the back of the wagon and climbed up beside him without saying a word. He urged Old Cookie forward, and they pulled out into the dirt street.

Mary Elizabeth was so furious with him that she didn't even realize when they pulled up in front of the bank. "Thank you for letting me use the wagon."

John Mills stepped out of the wagon and looked up at her. "No need to thank me, Mary Elizabeth," he said arrogantly. "This wagon isn't going *anywhere*. If you want that mudsill taking you to the stage, he'll have to supply his own wagon. But Eugene Smythe is still available." He smiled a fake smile at her and walked into the bank, leaving her sitting in the wagon wondering what she should do.

It didn't take her long, as there was only one thing *to* do—see if Ryan could come up with a wagon to get her to the stage. She shook her head, sighed, and climbed out of the wagon. Determined not to let her father ruin her plans, she put her head up and walked confidently across the street and into Ralston General Store to see Ryan.

"Ryan?" she said, as she walked through the door.

Ryan jumped out from the back room, with a paint brush in his hand and a smear of blue paint across his cheek. "Yes? Hi, Mary Elizabeth! Are you ready? I just need a minute." He started walking into the back room where he had come from, but she called him back out.

"Ryan, I have a problem. I was wondering if you could help me?" She walked up to the counter and tried to smile, but she was too nervous to do that.

"Anything, Mary Elizabeth, anything."

"Do you by any chance have access to a wagon? My father," ahem, she cleared her throat, "won't let me use his wagon."

"Oh! Is that all! Of course! I use a wagon to get supplies. Are you ready to go now? Let me just get cleaned up, and I'll go get it!" Ryan smiled broadly and disappeared into the back.

His smile and easy manner relaxed her. There was something about Ryan that always made her feel safe. And what more could a woman ask for than that? But

31

there was more. He had stolen her heart. Could she, no spring chicken that she was, ever hope to win a man like Ryan? Probably not, but at least she could spend some pleasant time with him before she found out that he wasn't interested in her.

"I'll be outside with my suitcase, Ryan!" she called to him.

"I won't be long, Mary Elizabeth. See you in a few minutes! Will you flip the sign on the door when you leave, please?"

Before Mary Elizabeth could even answer, she heard Ryan leave out the back door. She flipped the sign on the door so it said "Closed," but she didn't lock the door. Ryan always left the door open in case anybody needed anything. She had been inside when the store was closed and had left money on the counter. That's what everybody did. That's the kind of town Red Bluff was. It wasn't something anyone did in Atlanta. When a store was closed, you waited until it opened again. And if you desperately needed something and couldn't wait—you were just out of luck.

She stepped out the door with a big smile on her face. Ryan's cheerful attitude was contagious. Then she saw the curtain on the bank's window move. Her father. He had been watching. Her smile faded, and she walked across the street to retrieve her suitcase.

She was lifting it out of the wagon when her father approached. "So the mudsill was able to come up with a wagon, huh?"

Mary Elizabeth didn't even look at him. "He's not a mudsill."

He grabbed her hand and stuffed some money into it. "You'll need this for your trip and to rent a place after you get the job."

"Thank you." She stuffed the money into her handbag.

"I still don't like this, Mary Elizabeth. It's a long, lonely road to the stage. What if he . . . does something to you?"

"The only thing he's going to do is take me to the stage," she said flatly.

"I don't like it!"

"What do you want? Do you want him to report back when he returns to town?"

"Why don't you just send me a telegram when you get there?"

That would have been easy enough to do, but Mary Elizabeth was so angry that she wasn't going to agree to anything that he suggested. "I'm not sending a telegram!" She stuck out her hand, palm up. "Give me your albert!"

"What in tarnation do you want my albert for?"

"I'll give it to Ryan after I arrive safely. I'll just tell him that I need to return it to you. He won't know that you're checking up on him."

Her father pulled his watch out of his pocket and unfastened the chain from the buttonhole. He worked at the chain for a minute and looked up. "I can't get it disconnected from the watch. You'll have to think of something else."

She picked up her suitcase. "If you want to know that I arrived there safely, give me the dratted watch!"

"And *you* watch your language, young lady."

Turning to walk away, she said, "Have it your way, Father."

"Wait! Here's the watch! Tell him to give it to me

33

immediately upon his return!"

"Yeah, fine." She slipped the watch into a pocket on her dress. "Good-bye. See you in a few days. I'll send a telegram when I arrive back, and you can send *Eugene* to pick me up." She wasn't going to fight with him again over who would pick her up. At least she would be able to ride one way with Ryan. That would have to be enough.

"Mary Elizabeth? If you get the job, you'll send me a telegram from Farmtown to send your clothes, right?" her father asked in a pleading tone.

"Yes, Father, of course," said Mary Elizabeth without looking at him. Her father *and* her mother would like nothing better than for her to accept that teaching job. It had been her mother's idea from the beginning. And Mary Elizabeth had just gone along with it. But the idea that had taken root before was beginning to feel better and better. And the new idea made her smile.

CHAPTER EIGHT

RYAN DIDN'T KNOW whether or not they were in a hurry to get to the stage. When he had taken Eliza and Samuel, their stage hadn't left until the following morning; but he didn't know if every stage left on that schedule. He didn't even know where Mary Elizabeth was going. Or why. So, in case she was in a hurry, he trotted over to the livery to get his wagon.

"Ezra! Ezra!" Ryan called, as he ran into the livery.

"Yes, Ryan! Right here, what do you need?" said Ezra, running from the back where he was mucking a stall.

"I need to get my wagon. Can you help? I'll get Dolly. She's here, isn't she?"

"Yeah, she's here. But you usually don't go on Wednesdays."

"Special day, Ezra, special day!" Ryan grabbed some brushes and walked into Dolly's stall. Doing a quick but thorough job, he had finished brushing her when Ezra returned saying that the wagon was ready. Ryan walked Dolly out to the back where Ezra kept the wagons. Then Ezra helped him get Dolly into place and slipped the halter off Dolly.

"You're all set, Ryan. Safe travels!"

"Thanks, Ezra. Let's go, Dolly."

Dolly walked out of the barn and started going to the left—their usual direction when Ryan went back to the new Red Bluff. But today, he moved the reins and directed her straight. Dolly wasn't his horse. She was Jenna's horse, but she was also the horse that Granny rode whenever she needed to go anywhere. It was only once in a great while, but still, Ryan felt like he needed to check with her before he took the old woman's transportation away. He stopped Dolly when they got to the hotel. Then he jumped out of the wagon and ran into the hotel.

"Granny! Granny!"

"What is it, Grandson? What is it? What's all the shouting about?" Granny strolled out of Eliza's sitting room. She and her husband, Edward, were living there while Eliza and Samuel were back East.

"Granny, do you need Dolly today?"

"I *always* need Dolly—she's the sweetest horse around—but I don't need to ride her today, if that's what you're asking." Granny walked to the window, brushed the curtain aside, and waved to Dolly.

"Thanks, Gran!" Ryan kissed her on the cheek and walked quickly toward the door.

"Ohhh! I get it now, Grandson. This is about that woman, isn't it?" Granny smiled at Ryan.

He smiled back without saying a word, skipped the few steps to the wagon, jumped in, and encouraged Dolly down the street. Mary Elizabeth, seeing that the wagon was in front of the hotel, had started walking toward him. Ryan held up his hand for her to stop, and then a few horse steps later, asked Dolly to stop. Then Ryan jumped back out of the wagon, took the suitcase out of Mary Elizabeth's hand, and hoisted it into the back of the wagon. Then he took her hand and helped her into the wagon.

After climbing up in the seat next to Mary Elizabeth, Ryan asked Dolly to move forward. As they went by the bank, Ryan noticed that her father was watching them from the window. He was going to wave, but since Mary Elizabeth didn't, he thought that he shouldn't either. Mary Elizabeth moved around in the seat, adjusting herself.

"Are you okay? Isn't it comfortable enough for you?" Ryan asked, concerned.

"I've never sat in a more comfortable wagon in my life! Where did you get such a thing?"

Ryan laughed. "I just bought a regular wagon from Ezra at the livery, but then Nick and I made it a little more comfortable by padding the seat and the back. Since I use it all the time to go get supplies, I wanted something that I didn't dread sitting in. I'm glad you like it."

"I really do! Now I'm glad that my fa—that the other wagon didn't work out. This will make for a much more comfortable journey."

She smiled at him, and her face was so full of light that he almost dropped the reins right there. He would have loved to paint her right now, with her face in the light like that, with that smile. Regretfully, he said, "Glad you like it, Mary Elizabeth."

The next few miles went by in silence, a comfortable silence. It was something that Ryan wasn't used to. Most of the girlfriends in his life—all of them, in fact—were all big talkers. They did the talking, and he did the listening. He thought he liked it that way. But now, in the

37

silence between them, he realized that it was so much more enjoyable than hearing a woman talk about herself all the time.

He did want to know more about her, though. "Mary Elizabeth, where are you going on the stage?"

"Oh," she said and sounded like she was reluctant to talk about it. "I'm going for a job interview—at a school."

Ryan felt disappointed. Now that he finally had a chance to spend some time with her, she might accept a job in another city. What kind of irony was that? "You didn't want to work at the school here in town?"

"I was too late. By the time I knew that Annie was leaving, Rachel had already taken her place."

"That's too bad."

"Not really."

"You don't like Red Bluff?"

"Mostly, I do. But I really want to be a writer, not a school teacher."

Ryan perked up. "A writer? Really? That's really great!"

She looked at him. "Do you think so? My mother and father discourage me every chance they get. It was Mother's idea for me to apply for this job."

"Well, personally, I would say that you should definitely become a writer and, you know, not leave town." Ryan smiled at her, and when she turned to look at him, he shyly turned away.

"You know, it's funny. I had been planning all this time to accept the job if they offered it. But when my fa— when something came up at home, I began to realize that it was what my mother and father wanted for me, and not what I wanted for myself.

"I never imagined myself a teacher," she continued, "and would never have even considered this job if my mother hadn't kept pushing me. I've always wanted to be a writer. It's what I went to college for."

"You went to college?" Ryan asked, looking shocked.

"Oh, um, yeah, I did."

"Did you graduate?"

Mary Elizabeth nodded. "With honors."

Ryan shook his head. "I'm surprised. I didn't think women went to college in the nineteenth century—I mean," Ryan realized his mistake too late.

"Nineteenth century? That's a funny thing to say! Actually, some women do go to college. There were five of us when I started, but only two of us graduated."

"What happened to the other three?"

"They got married, got pregnant, and quit school."

Ryan was silent for a few minutes, and then said, "Well, I'm glad you didn't get married."

"I almost did. My father wanted me to marry Teddy Thornhill. He was pretty insistent about it and was extremely upset when I turned Teddy down." She shrugged. "But I didn't love him."

"Mary Elizabeth."

"Yes?"

"I was wondering if I could court you?" Ryan kept his head straight forward, reins in his hand, watching the dirt road in front of Dolly.

CHAPTER NINE

AFTER SHE HAD told him that she graduated from college, and he was silent for several minutes, Mary Elizabeth thought that he was just another man who wasn't interested in a woman who went to college. She had heard all the insulting comments: "She's too smart for her own good." "Once they're book-larned, they'll never make a good wife." And there were more. When Ryan was silent, she was afraid that's what he was thinking. And then he asked the question that she had hoped for—hoped for far too long.

Breathless, she said, "Yes!" She didn't want him to change his mind.

Ryan nodded his head and looked at her. "Good. Good. Should I ask your father first or something?"

"No! I mean, no, that's not necessary, Ryan. I'm twenty-five years old now." As soon as she said it, she regretted it. Twenty-five years old and not married—he's bound to wonder why she wasn't married—but she had said it, and it was too late now.

Ryan nodded his head, looked at her, and said, "I'd be happy to ask him, but if you're sure you don't want me to, then I won't."

"I'm sure, yes, I'm sure." The words couldn't come out fast enough. She couldn't even begin to imagine what would happen if Ryan approached her father and asked to court her. Because a simple "no" would never satisfy her father. It would be downright war. It would be awful.

After that, miles went by in silence. Mary Elizabeth wondered if maybe Ryan had changed his mind, and then chided herself for being silly. She had no reason at all to think such a thing. It was just that she had heard "spinster" and "not a spring chicken" too often for it not to affect her. She was indoctrinated is what she was. Completely indoctrinated.

Some time later, she began wondering about what her father had said about Ryan—that he was a mudsill. Although she really didn't think that he was, there was only one way to find out. "So, Ryan, have you, um, been to school?"

He looked at her and smiled. "You must mean college, right? Because now, almost everyone—oops, yes, I gradu-ated college. In art. I have an art degree."

Mary Elizabeth muttered to herself, "I *knew* he wasn't a mudsill!" She didn't think he heard her. But he did.

"What? I'm sorry, I didn't hear you."

"Um, well, I said that I knew you weren't a mudsill."

"What's a mudsill?" Ryan looked at her puzzled.

Mary Elizabeth laughed. "You went to college, but you don't know what a mudsill is? That's just plain silly!"

Ryan tilted his head, smiled at her, and sighed. "You look beautiful when you laugh."

Mary Elizabeth smiled shyly and rested her head on her chest. She wasn't really a shy person, but no one—including Teddy Thornhill—had ever complimented her like that. And she liked it.

After a few minutes of silence, Ryan glanced sideways at her, reached out, and squeezed her hand. Then he resumed holding the reins as if nothing at all had happened. Mary Elizabeth felt ecstatic. She had accidentally told Ryan how old she was, and he still seemed to like her! She sighed and blinked to keep tears from forming in her eyes. Although she didn't know whether this friendship with Ryan would go any further, right now she was just grateful for what he had given her already. Obviously, the "no spring chicken" did not apply to her. Or else Ryan didn't care about spring chickens!

They spent the rest of the trip in companionable silence. When the town appeared in the distance, Ryan turned toward her. "Well, Mary Elizabeth, I really hope you don't accept that job."

She looked at him with warmth in her eyes. "I don't even know why I'm going there. But if I don't, my parents would both have a conniption fit! I'll see you again, soon." This time, she didn't know where the courage came from, but she reached out and squeezed *his* hand.

Ryan stopped the wagon in front of the hotel as she had indicated, helped her out, and then lifted her suitcase out of the back. "Did you want me to pick you up?"

She took the suitcase from him and looked up into the bluest eyes she had ever seen. "Oh, yes—I mean no. My father will pick me up when I return."

"Okay. You'll let me know when you're back then? So, you know, we can begin courting."

Mary Elizabeth blushed. "Okay, Ryan, yes, I'll let you know." She turned and began walking into the hotel. Suddenly, she remembered and turned back. "Ryan, wait!" Reaching into her pocket, she pulled out her father's watch and held it out to him. "I accidentally took my father's watch. Can you give it back to him when you get back to your store?"

Wondering if he would notice the deceit, she watched him carefully. But he took the watch with a smile and then walked around the wagon. Looking up, he smiled and waved at her one more time before climbing into the seat, giving the reins a slight shake, and moving along down the street.

The hotel door opened and an older gentleman stepped out. "Ma'am," he said, as he held the door open for her. After one more glance at Ryan, she walked through the door and up to the front desk.

CHAPTER TEN

AFTER GETTING DOLLY a drink of water at the far edge of town, Ryan turned the wagon around for the long trip home, alone. When he drove past the hotel, he tried to look in, but there was no sign of Mary Elizabeth. He missed her already.

Ryan smiled when he thought about Mary Elizabeth squeezing his hand. She likes me, he thought. She really likes me! He started singing, "She likes me! She likes me!" Repeating it over and over, until Dolly slowed down and looked back at him, as if to say, "Dude! That's not singing!"

"Listen, Dolly," he said, "I'm an artist, not a singer, so deal with it!" Dolly turned forward again and spontaneously began to trot. "Trying to get it over with as soon as possible, huh, girl? Okay, I'll stop." He stopped singing, and Dolly slowed down to a fast walk. When Ryan started humming, Dolly broke into a trot again. "How about if I whistle?" When he tried whistling a few notes and Dolly didn't slow down, Ryan finally said, "Okay, we'll have it your way. I'll just sing in my head!" After a couple of minutes of silence, Dolly slowed down again. Ryan just shook his head. "I have to have a horse who thinks she's a voice critic." Dolly nickered and continued a fast walk.

The rest of the trip, Ryan thought and thought about what kind of "courting" they were going to do. As much as he'd like to take her out on the town—the new Red Bluff town, that is—he knew it was way too early for that. He'd have to be careful about that, anyway, because he didn't want to scare her off with tales about the future. The truth of it was there just weren't that many options in the nineteenth century. When he arrived back in Red Bluff a few hours later, he still hadn't come up with anything.

Dolly knew the way back to the livery, and Ryan had no reason to stop at the store first. Although he did notice Mary Elizabeth's father standing outside the bank looking around. When he looked right at Ryan as Dolly walked by, Ryan smiled and waved to him, and then continued to the livery.

As Ryan drove up in front of the place, Ezra walked out and held onto the reins while Ryan stepped off. "I'll take care of everything from here, Ryan," said Ezra.

"Thanks, Ezra!" Ryan reached into his pocket, glanced at the silver dollar to check the date and then handed it to Ezra. "I appreciate it, Ezra!"

He walked back to the store, but before he walked inside, he remembered the watch that Mary Elizabeth had given him, so he crossed the street. When he saw that Mary Elizabeth's father was still outside, Ryan smiled at him. But instead of a return smile, he received an ugly sneer.

"You were supposed to come directly to me when you arrived in town!" John Mills said, as he held out his hand.

Ryan, nonplussed by the man's anger, put the watch into the man's hand and said, "Sir, Mary Elizabeth asked me to give you the watch after I returned to my store, *not* when I arrived into town. And since I have not been to my store yet, I am actually giving you the watch *early*." He wanted to say, "You're welcome!" in a bitter tone and walk away, but this man could have an impact on his courting Mary Elizabeth, so Ryan just stood there. It was a good choice. Obviously the man wasn't used to people standing up to him.

"Oh, well, very well then. Thank you," he said quietly and walked back into the bank.

Ryan, breathing deeply to quell his own anger, watched him go before returning to his store. He walked inside and directly to the counter. There he found seven dollars and forty-four cents, and a list of items that had been purchased while he was gone. Smiling, Ryan put the money into the cash box and said, "Life in the nineteenth century is just too awesome." And to himself, he thought that the only thing missing was a woman in his life, and with any luck, that wouldn't be missing too much longer.

Then he had a thought that made his smile fade. What if she accepted the job in the city? What if she never returned? What if she really didn't like him? What if he never saw her again? Closing his eyes, he decided that instead of worrying about all the bad things that could happen, he should focus on the good. So he thought, what if she returns in just a couple days? What if she really likes him? What if they get married and live happily ever after? Ryan smiled. Those thoughts felt much better. And feeling good and thinking good thoughts were a much more positive way to live. He felt that for anything to happen between him and Mary Elizabeth, he had to continue thinking good thoughts.

CHAPTER ELEVEN

THE SWAYING MOTION of the stagecoach was putting Mary Elizabeth to sleep. She hadn't slept well the night before due to her going over in her mind every inch of the journey with Ryan. Everything he said, everything she said, and wondering if she could have spoken or acted differently. But she finally convinced herself that it had ended up all right, regardless. He still wanted to court her. That made her smile.

There were only five other people in the coach with her—a blessing because there was room for nine. It still felt like close quarters inside, and she couldn't imagine three more people squished inside there. They had all made each other's acquaintance in the first few minutes of the trip. There was a middle-aged woman, crying, dressed in black, and accompanied by a young man in his early teens, who kept his arm around her and looked as if he would break into tears any moment. Apparently her husband had just died, and she was returning to the city to be with her family. The woman and the boy sat on the same side of the coach as Mary Elizabeth.

On the other side were a newly married couple on

their bridal tour. They had eyes only for each other and kept whispering in each other's ears. Just watching them made Mary Elizabeth long to be back in Red Bluff with Ryan. She wondered if that could ever happen for them. She wondered if her father would ever allow it—not that it would matter, but it would make it easier. Next to the married couple was a man dressed in ragged and smelly clothing. He was so old that she hoped that he wouldn't die on the trip. It would only delay her returning to Red Bluff.

And that thought made her wonder why she was even on this stage coach to begin with. She had already firmly decided not to take the job that she had never wanted in the first place. So why was she even making the long trip out to Farmtown to apply for the job? Unfortunately, she knew the answer to that question. Her mother almost more than her father would be furious if she didn't at least go to the interview. Of course, if she didn't accept the job, there would still be anger and recriminations. But she could handle those better than she could handle not seeing where—if anywhere—Ryan's courting her will go.

Mary Elizabeth could not get him off her mind. And frankly, she was tired of thinking of him! Well, perhaps that wasn't exactly true. Perhaps it wasn't true at all. But still, she decided to try to set her mind on her surroundings. They were riding in a Wooden Concord stagecoach —the same kind her family rode in for many miles on their journey from Atlanta to Red Bluff. They took the train where they could, but there were many stretches where the train didn't go. So she was used to riding in a stagecoach, living in hotels or worse.

The horses pulling the coach—there were six of them

49

—were stout animals made for pulling heavy loads. They had large chests and thick legs, nothing like her dainty little mare, Cookie. How that horse made it across country was a miracle. She rode in a cattle car when they rode the trains and followed behind when they rode in a stagecoach. Her father and her mother wanted to leave Cookie behind, but Mary Elizabeth insisted that she must go. It wasn't until she crossed her arms and refused to leave without Cookie, that her father finally relented.

The man driving the coach held six lines in his hands —one for each horse. He was an old grizzled cowboy named Charlie, who acted gruff, but she had seen him gently wipe the tears from the crying woman's face before he helped her up into the coach. He probably had to act tough to do his job properly and so people wouldn't take advantage of him.

Mary Elizabeth looked out the window at the tall hills and the grasslands. The hills were mostly behind them now, with flatter ground ahead. She fell asleep to the swaying of the coach and with the blue skies above. Several hours later, she awoke with a start when the coach stopped suddenly. Old Charlie popped his head in the window. "Sorry for the delay, but one of the horses is limping. It will just take a minute to check."

She stuck her head out the window but he was on the other side of the coach, so she couldn't see anything. A few minutes later, he stuck his head back in the window holding up a large stone. "I think I caught it soon enough that it didn't do any damage. We should be fine now, and it won't be much longer." Then without so much as a smile, he climbed into his seat at the front of the coach, and they started to move forward once again.

By the time they arrived in the city, although she had

50

slept for hours, Mary Elizabeth still felt exhausted from the trip. The woman was still crying, and the old man was still alive. They had arrived safely, and Mary Elizabeth's only regret was that she was "forced" to take the trip at all when it wasn't what she wanted in the slightest. She checked into the hotel, got her clothes ready for the next day's interview, and fell immediately to sleep.

CHAPTER TWELVE

THE DAY AFTER taking Mary Elizabeth to the stage, Ryan was busy with customers all day. Although some of them came in the day before when they couldn't wait and left money for him on the counter, most of those who just needed to do some shopping waited until the store was open. Also, those who needed help with something or needed to order something special waited for him to be there. Since he had started "importing" items from the twenty-first century, there was a lot of special ordering going on. He lost money on all those items—buying them at twenty-first-century prices and selling them for nineteenth-century prices—but he didn't mind. With the added income of the valuable coins, Ryan was still way ahead. He didn't make as much money here as he did with his art store in the new Red Bluff, but he didn't need as much money, either. And he loved living here in the "past." And he would love it even more once he started courting Mary Elizabeth.

The following day started with Ryan wondering how soon she would return. She just left, he told himself. You dumb ninny, you never asked her when she was coming home! She would have made the trip and arrived already, and today she would probably have her interview at the school, he calculated. Would she accept the job? Would they give her an offer that she couldn't refuse? No, he decided. If she was a writer in her heart and soul, nothing could dissuade her from doing what she had to do. His art was that way. It was almost something out of his control. It wasn't that he wanted to paint —although he did—but it was more like he *had* to paint. He thought that writing would be that way, too.

If she truly had to write, then she would never accept a job as a teacher. She even said that applying for the job was her mother's idea. Besides, if it was any indication of how she felt about him, she did squeeze his hand before getting out of the wagon. That must mean something. Didn't it? Or was he putting too much stock into one simple action? He hoped not. He really hoped that she liked him as much as he liked her.

It had been a quiet morning, allowing Ryan the luxury of thinking about Mary Elizabeth. But now the door burst open and Nick walked in. "Hey, bud. Where'd ya go the other day? You were gone all day."

"Hey, Nick. I took Mary Elizabeth to catch the stage. It was a long trip."

"Was it a worthwhile trip, though?" Nick winked at Ryan.

Ryan smiled shyly. "Yeah, well, she consented to let me court her!"

"But where was she going on the stage?" Nick picked up a couple packets of nails and put them on the counter.

"To an interview for a school teacher. She said she didn't want to take the job, though. I'm hoping she

53

doesn't."

Nick plunked some coins on the counter. "I just love these nineteenth-century prices!"

"What are you working on now?"

"Getting some work done on Jenna and Josiah's ranch. Fixing the barn to her specifications and fencing in the pasture." Nick took the change that Ryan handed him and slipped it into his pocket. "So you're going to court her, huh? Does this mean that you're ready to settle down?"

Ryan turned away from Nick. "Um, well, I, uh—"

"You are! You're thinking of settling down with her! Since I've known you, and I've known you forever, that has never *ever* been in your mind before. Wow, I'm impressed."

"Well, you know, she has something to say about it, too."

"Dude! This is the nineteenth century! It's more like her family has something to say about it."

"Yeah, but she's twenty-five years old. You know, her own person."

"No, no," said Nick, shaking his head. "As long as she's living at home, she's under her parents'—mainly her father's—rule. And young women in these days only very rarely lived on their own. So what her father says, goes. If I were you, I'd try to get on his good side, or there will be no courting her at all."

"She asked me not to ask her father if I could court her."

Nick raised his eyebrows. "Drama, dude. It sounds like drama to me. I'd stay away if I were you."

Ryan smiled. "Glad I'm not you, Nick. I'm going for it. I really *really* like this girl."

"If she's twenty-five, she's no girl, Ryan. In these days, if a woman is twenty-five and not married, she's practically an old maid."

Before Ryan could answer, the door opened and his sisters, Kat and Jenna, walked in, giggling, with Jenna carrying her new baby. When they walked up to the counter, Nick said, "Ladies," he nodded his head and then smiled at the baby, Milo, "Gentleman," then he walked to the door. "See ya later, Ryan. Good luck."

"Good luck with what?" asked Jenna, never one to leave an opening like that alone.

Ryan stepped up to the baby and tickled him under the chin. Milo smiled, and Ryan wondered if it was still gas at that age, or if the baby was really smiling at him. "Well, um, yeah, well, I've decided to start courting Mary Elizabeth."

"Ryan! A real woman, and not just a pretty face! You know she's a college graduate, right?" Kat was smiling broadly. She had changed so much since she had moved here to the nineteenth century and married the doctor.

"Yes, I know."

"So where are you going to take her? Supper at the hotel?" asked Jenna, grabbing some organic baby food that Ryan always had on hand especially for her.

"I was thinking I'd rather do something else. But I don't know what. It's these times. I love it here, but they're so limiting."

"I have the perfect idea!" Jenna wiped some slobber off Milo's face. "You'll come to supper at my house. It will be like a double date. That's the kind of thing that's done in these times. It's perfectly acceptable." Jenna looked satisfied with herself for the suggestion.

Ryan nodded. "You know, I think that might work."

Then he remembered what Josiah had said. "Oh, no, Jenna, I don't think that would be a good idea at all."

"Whyever not? It's perfect!"

Ryan shook his head. "Oh, no, I don't think it's perfect at all."

Jenna tilted her head and looked at him. "Oh! You mean because Josiah asked her out?"

"He told you?" Although Ryan knew his sister and her husband were close, that surprised him.

"Of course he told me! We share everything!"

"You don't think it would be weird?"

"Ryan, it was nothing. He asked her to supper, and she said no. He was already in love with me and trying not to be. Case closed. So, when would you like to come? Tonight?"

Relieved, Ryan shrugged. "Mary Elizabeth is out of town. I don't know when she'll be back."

"Where did she go?" asked Kat.

"To a job interview in Farmtown. A teacher. But she doesn't want to be a teacher."

"Then why did she go?" asked Kat, who rarely did anything that she didn't specifically want to do.

"It's these times, Kat," said Jenna. "Women have expectations to live up to. Parental pressure. It sucks, really." Turning to Ryan, she added, "When she does return, you let me know, and I'll fix us a great supper."

She paid Ryan for the baby food, and then she and Kat walked back out of the store, giggling like school girls.

CHAPTER THIRTEEN

MORNING CAME TOO early after the rough journey the day before. Mary Elizabeth still felt shaken from the trip. She quickly dressed and walked downstairs. Unlike the hotel in Red Bluff, this hotel had no restaurant. There was, however, a suitable cafe next door. After a satisfying breakfast of eggs and fried ham, she returned to the hotel to wait.

The principal of the school, a Miss Prosser by name, had arranged to have transportation for her. She had explained to her by letter that this was not normally done, but due to Mary Elizabeth's having come so far and having no transportation of her own, plus Mary Elizabeth's *considerable* education, they would make an exception in her case. Mary Elizabeth, remembering the correspondence, rolled her eyes. Her mother had written the initial letter to Miss Prosser and had no doubt gone on and on about how well-educated Mary Elizabeth was. Although it was true, she was well-educated, she still felt sure that her mother had exaggerated her accomplishments. Regardless, here she was, about to interview for a job that she had no interest in—and no intention of accepting.

She had just stepped back into the hotel after her breakfast when a wagon pulled up outside, the driver squinting to see in the windows of the hotel. The man was dressed in work clothes, and there was lumber stacked in the back of the wagon. It made Mary Elizabeth laugh. It wasn't that she expected a coach and four like Cinderella, but she didn't expect this either! Walking outside and suppressing her laughter, she said, "Are you looking for me? Mary Elizabeth Mills?"

"Yes, Ma'am, I am! Climb aboard!" The man smiled at her but didn't offer to help.

She hoisted her skirt and stepped up, grasping the man's outstretched hand. "Thank you!" she said cordially. Then she noticed that her skirt had gotten caught on a nail on the side of the wagon. Leaning down, she unhooked it from the nail and looked at the damage. It had torn the edge of her skirt, and part of it was hanging down. Oh, well, she thought, there was nothing she could do about it now.

The man nodded and shook the reins, and the horse moved down the road. The buildings passed slowly by. Mary Elizabeth shivered. It had the feeling of Atlanta, and didn't feel at all like Red Bluff. Although she had missed Atlanta when she left, she had grown accustomed to the small town feel of Red Bluff. She realized she missed it. She missed Ryan, more, though.

"How far is it to the school?" she asked.

"Not too far. It's just a few blocks away—it used to be the jail!"

"The jail? You mean the cells are now the classrooms?" The thought of it made her shiver again.

"Yup. Yeah, well, we tore out the walls between two

58

cells for the classrooms. And of course put in walls and regular doors instead of the bars," he laughed and then continued. "But you can still tell it was a jail when you're in there, you know? It's got that *feeling* to the place."

Mary Elizabeth nodded. "Yes, I imagine it would."

They rode for the next few minutes in silence, until the man adjusted the reins and the horse stopped. "Here we are. Go through that front door, go to the hallway, turn left, and it's the first office on the right. That's Miss Prosser. That's who you're supposed to see, right?"

"Yes, that's right."

"Yeah, that's what I figured. She's the one who sent me to pick you up. And I'll be the one to return you to the hotel when you're finished."

Mary Elizabeth climbed carefully down from the wagon, careful not to catch her skirt on the nail again. "Thank you for the ride. See you later, then." She waved to him, and he shook the reins and was off.

After following his instructions, she found herself in front of a closed door, with a sign on it that said "Miss Prosser, Principal." She wondered if she should knock or just walk in. Looking down at her torn skirt, she shrugged and knocked on the door.

Miss Prosser opened the door and frowned. "Miss Mills, I presume?"

"Yes." Mary Elizabeth nodded her head and smiled.

Miss Prosser motioned for her to come in, and as Mary Elizabeth walked by, Miss Prosser looked her up and down. "Your skirt is torn," she said without preamble.

"Yes, I'm sorry. It got caught on a nail on the wagon you sent for me."

"Frankly, Miss Mills, I expected more from a college

graduate. You *are* a college graduate, aren't you?"

Mary Elizabeth, flustered at the woman's accusation and tone of voice, said, "Yes, of course I am. I thought my mother sent you a copy of my degree."

The woman thumbed through some paperwork on her desk. "Oh, yes," she frowned, "here it is." She tapped the document twice with her finger and then squinted her eyes at Mary Elizabeth. "What exactly did you major in?"

"English."

"And where was this college that you went to?" Miss Prosser demanded.

Mary Elizabeth had already had enough of this treatment. "Atlanta. You know, the city in Georgia?" she said innocently, as she smiled sweetly at Miss Prosser.

"Of course I know Atlanta, Georgia! What do you take me for? A mudsill? I may not have graduated college, but I'm quite educated!"

Ah, thought Mary Elizabeth, so that's it then. She's afraid I'll take over her job as principal! She smiled. Maybe she wouldn't have to turn down a job offer after all. She may not even get a job offer! "Oh, sorry, I thought maybe you hadn't read the degree." Smiling at Miss Prosser, Mary Elizabeth nodded toward her degree.

"Yes, well," said Miss Prosser, straightening the papers on her desk. "What did you say you majored in?"

"English."

"Why would you major in English if you wanted to be a school teacher?"

"I majored in English because I'm a writer."

"A writer? Are you published, then?"

"Um, uh, no, not yet."

"Well then. I guess you're not a writer, then, are you?

And frankly, Miss Mills, I really can't see hiring someone who stutters. It wouldn't be right to expose the children to that sort of thing, don't you agree?"

Although Mary Elizabeth had a warning that it would come to this, she didn't expect stern and humorless Miss Prosser to insult her in a way that made her feel so vulnerable. She looked down at her hands and didn't answer. After a minute of silence, Miss Prosser stood up.

"I think we both realize that this job is not for you." Miss Prosser stood up, walked toward the door, and opened it.

Mary Elizabeth stood up and walked out the door without looking at Miss Prosser. "Thank you," she said. The woman may have been insulting and rude, but Mary Elizabeth didn't need to sink down to her level.

"Just wait out in front." Miss Prosser looked down at the torn skirt. "We don't want the students to get the wrong impression and think that this school would hire a —a—*hobo*." She turned around without another glance at Mary Elizabeth and closed the door of her office with a slam.

After more than an hour, while Mary Elizabeth shifted from one foot to the other, the man with the wagon finally showed up. She climbed into it, not paying any attention to the nail. Her dress tore even more. The man didn't say a word to her on the way back to the hotel. And it took all her strength to keep from crying—which even at the time she thought was strange because she didn't want the job anyway. But she felt devastated. She stumbled out of the wagon and ran into the hotel, the torn dress trailing behind her.

CHAPTER FOURTEEN

IT HAD BEEN an uneasy few days for Ryan. Wondering when Mary Elizabeth would return, wondering *if* she would return, and wondering if she *still* would consent to him courting her. He had never doubted himself with women before, but there had never been a woman like Mary Elizabeth—never a woman who mattered. Still, he got through the two days, painting and waiting on people who came into his store. And when Sunday came, he retrieved his wagon from the livery, and started on his weekly trip to the new Red Bluff to "import" more supplies. He had an idea for Mary Elizabeth and was eager to act on it—despite what might happen between them.

As Dolly made her way down the narrow path that led to the cave, Ryan noticed that the trail had become less and less hidden. Doc and Zack had camouflaged the trail into the cave from the other side, but he thought that this side should be camouflaged as well. After all these months of more and more folks coming and going, the trail was obvious. And it was that obvious-ness that could get them all in trouble. He made a mental note to get someone to help him cover it up.

Through the cave and down the rickety path Ryan and Dolly went. The new trail that Doc and Zack had created didn't include a path for wagons, so Ryan made his own path, a different one each week. After reaching the main trail, the path was easy going, and in no time, they had reached Jenna's ranch. It was where Ryan, Jenna, and Kat had all grown up, and where Jenna lived until she discovered the cave, moved back in time, and married Josiah. Now, Kat's daughter, Madison, and her boyfriend from the nineteenth century, Zack, lived there. And friends and relatives from the nineteenth century were constantly interrupting their lives by staying overnight or several nights in one of the spare rooms. Ryan wouldn't be spending the night, though. He wanted to get back home in case Mary Elizabeth had returned.

Dolly stopped at all the gates to let Ryan jump off and open them. He had even trained her to walk through on her own and stop on the other side, so he didn't have to climb back in and out of the wagon again to close said gate. She was a good girl. They made their way to the barn, and Ryan unhooked her from the wagon so she could roam in the pasture while he did his shopping.

Ryan walked to the front door, knocked, and called out, "You guys home or up or both?" A sleepy Zack, dressed in pajama bottoms and no top, opened the door for him.

"Ah, sorry, Ryan, we had a late night last night. See ya later. G'night." Zack stumbled back down the hall in the direction of his and Madison's room.

Ryan closed the door behind him and smiled. "Thanks, Zack!" Although Ryan knew that the door was probably unlocked, plus Ryan had his own key just in case, he would never barge into the house unannounced. Zack and Madison were young lovers, after all. It just wasn't a good idea.

It did disappoint Ryan, however, that Zack didn't pay him the money he owed him. Since Zack knew so much about coins and had become friends with the dealer, Ryan had made him a deal. Zack would take the coins that Ryan gave him, trade them in at the coin dealer, and keep ten percent of the profit. Then he would give Ryan half the profit in nineteenth-century money, and half in twenty-first-century money. Ryan needed the twenty-first-century money to buy the items that he'd then sell at his store in the nineteenth century.

When he first started doing that, he had considered the idea of charging the twenty-first-century transplants more money—the actual cost of the item. But he realized that would be a nightmare and would confuse any nineteenth-century person who may be at the store at the same time. Besides, Ryan had plenty of money, and there was one thing that he dearly loved about the nineteenth century: it was so much more about community than the twenty-first century. People really helped each other. People really cared about each other. And he liked that. It was one of the reasons he had chosen to stay, and one of the reasons that he would never return full-time to the twenty-first century.

Although Zack didn't pay him, Ryan had become prepared just in case. It wasn't the first time that Zack and Madison had a late night, so Ryan always brought enough money to buy what he needed. Now he jumped into his car—which he kept parked at the edge of the ranch with several other cars—and drove into town. First stop, thrift stores. There was something else that he had started doing at his store: he had begun taking orders for clothes that people wanted. Although most people made their own clothes—the women, that is—some people liked the idea of buying "store bought" clothes. So instead of Ryan ordering out of Denver which took forever to arrive in those days, he asked the people if they minded good quality used clothing that he could get much faster. Everyone agreed. And since nobody had many sets of clothes in those days—usually just two—there wasn't that much buying going on. The old Red Bluff was a small town, after all. So it wasn't that much of a bother, and Ryan loved the expression on their faces when they saw the "almost" new clothing. Today, the only things on his list were a couple of pairs of jeans and one shirt. But he was also looking for the item that he wanted for Mary Elizabeth. He wasn't sure that he would find it at a thrift store, and he was aware that he might have to look at an antique store to get the right one.

Ryan had found the jeans and the shirt at the first thrift store, but it wasn't until the third one that he had found exactly what he was looking for. He stuck it in his car and drove to the grocery store to pick up the final items that he'd bring back to the old Red Bluff. Inside his car was a large, square cooler. There was an identical one in the wagon—only he had built a plain wooden case around it, so no one would actually see the cooler. It got the job done.

CHAPTER FIFTEEN

AFTER TRYING AND failing to catch an earlier stage back home, Mary Elizabeth had spent an agonizing afternoon and night wondering why she had the reaction she did to Miss Prosser, when she didn't even want the job. The answer became obvious quickly, but its repercussions added to the agony. Miss Prosser had said that Mary Elizabeth wasn't a writer. And it hurt so much because Mary Elizabeth had started wondering the same thing. She hadn't written in—it was more than just months— could it possibly be years? That thought caused many tears to fall. When had she last written even a single word? And why had she stopped? Could the last piece she had written really be the journal that she had kept on their long journey from Atlanta to Red Bluff? She had told Ryan she was a writer, and she hadn't written any- thing in so long. Besides everything else, she was a liar! What hurt most of all, though, was that she wasn't a writer, after all.

Morning came too early after a rough night of almost no sleep, but she was grateful for it. She had telegraphed her father the previous day when she would be at the hotel. So she hoped he would arrange to have someone there the day after she arrived. There was nothing she wanted more than to spend the night in her own bed, in her own room, in Red Bluff. Walking downstairs, she inquired at the front desk about the stage. It was scheduled to leave really early.

"I'm sorry, Ma'am," the man told her, "the wheel was broken, and they have to fix it. Depending on how bad it is, it will take at least a couple of hours. Sorry."

Dejected at this unexpected and unwanted delay, she shuffled over to the cafe to have breakfast. Although she wanted to see Ryan—needed to see Ryan—her new loss of identity disturbed her. She choked down her eggs and bitter coffee. Looking out the window and across the street, and lamenting that she could no longer call herself a writer, an idea occurred to her. After paying for her meal, she rushed out of the cafe and across the street. In such a hurry, she didn't notice the wagon full of chickens coming down the road. The driver had to rein in his horses quickly so as not to run her over. He yelled at her, and the chickens continued to squawk after he drove on.

Mary Elizabeth strolled into the general store with a new sense of peace about her. After asking the clerk for what she needed, she picked up the items and set the coins on the counter to pay for them. Grateful that she had brought her larger handbag with her instead of the small reticule, she placed her newly purchased items inside. Smiling to herself, she looked up and down the street and crossed in confidence.

When she walked into the hotel, the clerk said, "Ma'am, good thing you're here. There wasn't that much trouble to the wheel. The stage will be leaving in fifteen minutes."

"Thank you!" Mary Elizabeth rushed upstairs, retrieved her already packed suitcase, and brought it back down. She paid her hotel bill, walked out the door, and sat down on the bench outside. For the first time in twenty-four hours, she had a smile on her face. As she waited for the coach, her mind drifted, and the general store across the street blurred into the thoughts inside her head.

When the stage pulled up a few minutes later, Mary Elizabeth thought the Concord stagecoach looked the same, but the horses were different and so was the driver. Of course all the Wooden Concord stagecoaches looked similar. The driver this time was a young man who couldn't keep still. He had set the brake on the wagon, jumped off, and started loading people's luggage into the back of the wagon. Clutching her newly acquired items tightly in her hand, she climbed inside the wagon. Although she didn't have a window seat this time, it didn't bother her. She had plenty to keep her mind and hands busy on this trip.

Unfortunately, unlike her trip over here, this time the coach was full. A fat man smelling of sweets sat next to her on one side, and a cringing woman sat on her other side. The woman acted as if she didn't want to be touched, an impossibility in the tight quarters. On the other side of the woman sat a slender man with his head against the side of the coach, already dozing off. Across from them, sat a family of four: a mother, a father, and two young teenage sons. Aside from the two boys occasionally pinching each other's legs, the family was quiet. And quiet was exactly what she needed right now, although she felt so enthusiastic about her new project that she didn't think it would matter.

She waited until the coach drove away from the city, and then she began. Pulling out the first pencil from her bag—she had bought many, just in case—she then pulled out the paper and began to write. With the jerking and swaying of the coach, it was difficult, but Mary Elizabeth was determined. After writing down the first few words, "It had started many years before" she had closed her eyes and smiled triumphantly. She was a writer again.

CHAPTER SIXTEEN

IT WAS ANOTHER false alarm. Ryan's neck was getting sore from turning quickly to look out the window whenever he heard a noise that might be a wagon coming into town bringing Mary Elizabeth home. He went over and over it in his head. He dropped her off Wednesday. She traveled Thursday, had the interview Friday, and he hoped that she started her return journey on Saturday—which meant that she should be home Sunday. But, although he had returned from the new Red Bluff early and had watched the window until candle-lighting, she had not returned on Sunday. He cringed to think that she might have accepted the job. Since he didn't believe that, though, he kept watching the window—and didn't get any painting done.

The door to the store opened, and Josiah strode in and up to the counter. "You're not painting."

Ryan frowned and shook his head. "I know, I know. I just can't focus right now." He shrugged. "And I can't see the front window from back there."

Josiah laughed. "Oh, you do have it bad, don't you?"

Ryan nodded. "I expected her back yesterday. I'm

wondering if she decided to stay."

"She said you could court her, though, right?"

"Yes, but she went away for a job interview." Ryan checked the window again.

"But she told you that she didn't want the job, right?"

Ryan grunted. "I'm just worried, man."

"She'll be here, don't worry. So when will you two come to supper?"

"She's not even back yet!"

Josiah reached out and squeezed Ryan's arm. "Ryan, plan the supper, and then she'll turn up. That's how it works. So when will you two come over?"

"Josiah, I just can't do it that way." He shook his head and checked the window.

"You know, now that you mention it, you're right. Did you say that she didn't want you to ask her father if you could court her?"

"Yes, she said that."

"Then it better be dinner and not supper. That way you can have her home before dark, and it won't create any problems at home."

"Problems? What do you mean?" He stole a quick glance out the window again.

"Supper would mean that you need a chaperone."

"Well, you and Jenna would be chaperones!"

"It doesn't work like that. Who would be your chaperone on the way over to our house and back into town?"

"Oh. Never thought of that. Well, I don't have to worry about it if she doesn't come home, now, do I?"

"You're impossible, Ryan!" Josiah shook his head. "By the way, Jenna told me that you didn't want to come to supper at our house because I had asked Mary Elizabeth out. That was real sweet of you, really. But Jenna and I tell each other everything. She already knew about Mary Elizabeth and about the school teacher that I had asked out."

"You mean Rachel?"

"No, no, it was before Rachel. You know, the one who married Henry Ralston—the guy you bought the store from."

"Oh, yeah, that's right."

"And it didn't bother Jenna?"

Josiah shook his head. "I was so in love with your sister from the first moment that I saw her—it just took me awhile to figure that out. And then when she told me *when* she was from, of course that scared me off, too." He nodded toward Ryan. "I'd be careful about that if I were you, Ryan, although you've been living here for a year now. That makes it a little different. She has no reason to think that you might return *there* permanently. I guess *that's* what I was afraid of."

Before Ryan could answer, he looked out the window again and saw a wagon come into view. Mary Elizabeth was sitting in it! "Josiah! She's here! She's here!" Ryan ran to the door, but as he opened it, he saw that her father had come out of the bank. Ryan stopped abruptly. Mary Elizabeth was escorted into the bank, with her father carrying her suitcase.

Disappointed, Ryan turned back to Josiah, but not before he saw the young man drive away in the wagon. "Who's that?"

Josiah looked out the window. "Oh, that's young Eugene Smythe."

"Why did he get to pick her up, I wonder, and not me?"

"His father works at the bank, Ryan. I'm sure it's

nothing. He's also only nineteen years old. I wouldn't worry about it. You know, I never realized how much of a worrier you were."

Just then, Ryan happened to notice Mary Elizabeth coming out of the bank and heading across the street. "Josiah! She's coming over here! Get out!"

"Yes, sir! Right away, sir! Man, a sheriff doesn't get any respect around here!" Josiah laughed as he slipped out the door in time to hold it open for Mary Elizabeth.

"Mary Elizabeth!" called out Ryan. "I was so worried! I expected you home yesterday, so I thought you accepted the job!"

She walked up to the counter and said, "Ryan, I wasn't even offered the job! And I didn't get home yesterday because my father was angry to have me back, so he made me wait."

"I'm so glad you're back, Mary Elizabeth." Ryan didn't want to get mushy, but he felt mushy. He felt so relieved at seeing her.

"I'm glad to be back, too. And I have something extraordinary to tell you!" She glanced out the window. "Oh, but I better go. I'm supposed to be getting the wagon."

"Let's go out the back way. I'll walk you down there." Ryan escorted her through the back of the shop to the rear door. As they walked outside, he said, "What's extraordinary?"

"Remember I told you that I was a writer?"

Ryan nodded. "Yes, of course."

"Well, I lied. I hadn't written anything in a long time —since my journal when we traveled cross-country to get here. But during the interview, which didn't go at all well by the way, the woman said that I was not a writer. I was devastated, because when I thought about it, I thought she was right. It had been so long since I'd written anything. So on my way home, in the bumpy stage coach, I wrote this." She opened her handbag, took out a bunch of loose papers, and shoved them into his hands.

"Wow! You wrote a lot!"

Standing in front of the livery, she said, "It's a novel based on our journey. I think it's going to be good. I'm sorry I told you that I was a writer when I really wasn't."

Ryan handed her back the papers and said, "Mary Elizabeth, once a writer, always a writer. You were just taking a break."

"A long break! Ryan, I have to bring the wagon to my father or he'll have a conniption fit. He's angry that I didn't get the job."

"Mary Elizabeth? When can I start courting you? Will you come to dinner with me to Jenna and Josiah's?"

Ezra had heard them talking and now brought the wagon, hitched to Old Cookie, outside the big barn. "Thanks, Ezra," said Mary Elizabeth. "Ryan, I'd love to! When?"

"How about tomorrow?"

"I think I could manage that! I'll see you then!"

Ryan helped her into the wagon and watched her drive down the dusty street. Then, with a huge smile on his face, he skipped back to his store.

CHAPTER SEVENTEEN

"Where were you?" demanded her father, who had climbed into the wagon after putting her suitcase in the back. He grabbed the reins out of her hands.

"I went to get the wagon, just like you told me."

He turned the wagon around so they were heading for home and glanced at Ryan's store. "Yes, of course you did. Tell me again why you did not get the job."

"I told you." Knowing this question was coming, Mary Elizabeth had decided to start from Miss Prosser's perspective. "The woman who interviewed me, Miss Prosser, didn't believe that I was a college graduate— even when Mama had sent her a copy of my degree. After she had ascertained that I really was—and she confessed that she wasn't—I believe that she feared for her job, and thus said I was not suitable for the position." Regardless of what else had happened at the interview, Mary Elizabeth sincerely believed this part was true. A hobo! The thought of it made Mary Elizabeth grimace.

"Well, we'll have to see what your mother has to say about this. She'll be extremely disappointed in you, Mary Elizabeth, as am I."

The next few minutes—the rest of the trip home—were spent in silence. But she didn't care what her mother had to say, and she didn't care if both of them were disappointed in her or not. All that mattered was that the following day, she was going to dinner with Ryan. Smiling, she closed her eyes momentarily, until her father stopped the wagon by the house.

She climbed out of the wagon, and her father handed her the suitcase. As she walked toward the house, her mother charged out the door and enveloped Mary Elizabeth in her arms.

"Mary Elizabeth!" she said nodding her head. "You got the job, right?"

"No, Mama, I did not."

"You didn't? That cannot be. What do you mean you didn't?"

Her father, after quickly parking the wagon and putting Old Cookie in the barn with a bunch of hay, walked past them into the house. "Let's discuss this tragedy over supper. I'm starved. C'mon inside."

Cora Mills walked straight to the kitchen to serve the meal. Mary Elizabeth put her suitcase into her room, then walked to the kitchen to help out.

"I still can't believe she didn't get the dratted job," grumbled her father. When he saw her, he said, "Mary Elizabeth, tell your mother what you told me."

After putting all the food onto the table and sitting down, Mary Elizabeth repeated her story about Miss Prosser. Then she put a forkful of chicken in her mouth and thought that would be the end of it. Unfortunately, it was only the beginning.

"No, no, I don't believe it. There has to be something else. Tell me everything, Mary Elizabeth, everything that happened at the interview." Her mother looked at her attentively from across the table.

Mary Elizabeth sighed, put her fork down, put her hand up to her mouth, and gazed into the nothingness across the room. "Okay, I'll tell you everything." She started from the nail and the torn dress, continued with Miss Prosser's fretful attitude, relayed the exact words of the interview, and finished with Miss Prosser escorting her out with the hobo comment and slamming the door on her. Although she held it together during the whole monologue, when she came to the end, she broke down in tears. It was unexpected, but although she had written pages and pages on her way home, the impudent accusation about not being a writer still disturbed her.

Cora Mills reached across the table and patted Mary Elizabeth's arm. "It's all right, dear. I will write a letter to the mayor and give him a complete report on how rudely you were treated. You'll get that job yet, dear, don't you worry."

"Mama, please don't do that," was all that Mary Elizabeth could get out between sobs.

"Let your mother take care of this, Mary Elizabeth. It's for the best," said John Mills.

Mary Elizabeth bit her lip to try to control her crying so she could speak. "No," she sobbed trying to catch her breath. "I don't want the job! I wouldn't have accepted the job had she offered it to me!"

"What?" asked her mother.

"What do you mean you wouldn't have accepted it? Of course you would have! I would have seen to it!" said her father, pounding his fist on the table.

"I do not want to be a school teacher!" she said. "I am *not* a school teacher!"

"No, Mary Elizabeth, you're worse! You're a spinster!" her mother said before knocking her chair over as she ran out of the room covering her face with her hands.

"Now see what you've done. You've made your mother cry." Her father glared at her.

She stood up and looked at her father. "Doesn't anybody care what *I* want?"

"What you want is irrelevant. You'll do what you *should* do; you'll do what you're *told* to do! Now go apologize to your mother and tell her that you'll take the job as soon as she arranges it for you."

"No, Papa. I won't apologize to her. If anything, she needs to apologize to *me*. And there is no way I'm going to take that job. I don't want it, and I won't take it!" She lifted her head and strode resolutely from the room.

"Listen to me, young lady." John Mills stood in the doorway and called after her. "You don't want that job? Fine. Then you find yourself another job in the next two weeks or you're not welcome in my house any longer!"

Mary Elizabeth, stunned, turned around to look at his angry face. "But there are no jobs around here."

John Mills narrowed his eyes and nodded. "You call yourself a writer? Then you better start writing letters to find a job for yourself. You have two weeks!" He turned around and walked back into the kitchen to finish his dinner.

Mary Elizabeth took a deep breath, walked slowly into her bedroom, and collapsed on the bed, tears streaming down her face.

CHAPTER EIGHTEEN

Ryan WAS BESIDE himself all morning. He and Mary Elizabeth had not discussed what time, he had just said "dinner" and she had accepted. So what time would she come over? Jenna had said that she would be prepared, regardless. And she encouraged him to try to relax. Josiah had arranged with Nick to watch the sheriff's office and had already left for home. Still, Ryan felt like something was undone. The typewriter! Of course! He hadn't gotten it ready yet.

It was a small, portable, manual of course, that he had found at the thrift store. At first, he had thought that he had to get an antique one that reflected the times. Then he realized that since they were so new, no one in the nineteenth century really knew what they were supposed to look like. Besides, who would see it? Not that many people. Although he liked to be careful about such things, he felt this was safe enough. He wrapped it in his saddlebags and put it where he wouldn't forget to take it.

At 11:50, Mary Elizabeth strolled into the store, looking a little bedraggled. "Mary Elizabeth, are you okay?"

She nodded reluctantly. "I was in my bedroom all

morning after a quarrel with my parents last night. So I neglected to ask my father to leave me the wagon—which meant that I had to walk all the way to town. Sorry if I'm late."

"You didn't have any breakfast then?" asked Ryan, concerned.

She shook her head. "No, but it's okay. We're eating soon, right?"

Ryan walked over to one of the tables and took an apple out of a small pile. "Here, eat this. It's already washed."

"Washed? What do you mean?"

Ryan shook his head and chided himself for his twenty-first-century thinking. Although he only brought organic apples to town, he still always washed them. "Oh, nothing. You ready? Let's go."

He grabbed the saddlebag and escorted her out the back door, and they walked to the wagon, which was already outside waiting. While Ryan stood by the wagon waiting to help her into it, Mary Elizabeth walked toward Dolly and stroked her face. "Hi, Dolly. Good to see you again, girl."

As Ryan helped her up, he said, "Do you like horses, Mary Elizabeth? Do you ride?"

"I used to ride all the time, but I haven't since I started college. My mother told me that I was too old for such juvenile foolishness, and that it wasn't proper for a young lady to ride horses. So I stopped, and after a while I didn't even think about it anymore."

"So you can ride, then."

"I haven't ridden for years, Ryan."

"But you used to like it, right?"

She nodded. "I loved it."

80

"Doesn't your father have a horse you can borrow?"

"He has a horse, but not one that I could borrow. Rojo is a stallion."

"Your father rides a stallion?"

"He said it helps him in his business. When people want to borrow money, he rides out to see them on his stallion. He says it makes them have more respect."

"That's crazy. Well, I'm sure Ezra has a horse you could borrow. Wouldn't you like to go riding sometime?"

She looked at him and cocked her head. "You know, that does sound like fun."

"Good. I think it sounds like fun, too. I know that people in this time don't usually ride for pleasure, but—"

"What do you mean 'this time'?"

"Oh, sorry. Nothing. I just mean that most people don't see entertainment in riding horses, but personally, I love it."

Mary Elizabeth looked to the side dreamily and sighed. "I used to love it."

"Well, you can again! Now tell me about your trip and what happened."

When she finished telling him every sordid detail of her trip, Ryan nodded and waited several minutes before answering. "Yes, I see what you mean, and I agree completely that Miss Prosser feared for her job. And I'm so sorry about her making you feel like you weren't really a writer." He reached over and squeezed her hand. "Like I said before, once a writer, always a writer. You had nothing to worry about. Especially now. Have you done any more with that story you were working on?"

She looked down. "No. I've been in a right pucker since the quarrel with my parents."

"Quarrel? Yeah, you mentioned that earlier. But it

wasn't like you turned the job down. She didn't offer it to you!"

"Mmmm. Yeah, but my mother was going to write a letter to the mayor complaining about everything and demanding that I get the job."

"Bummer."

"What?"

"I mean, yeah, that is too bad that she was going to do that. So you told her that you didn't want her to do that? Was that why they were mad?"

"I told her that I wasn't going to accept the job anyway, and that I wasn't a school teacher." Mary Elizabeth looked down at her hands. "That's when she called me a spinster and ran out of the room, crying."

"A spinster! You're too young to be a spinster! Oh, here we are. Ready for dinner? You'll love Josiah and Jenna. They are the greatest couple, and little Milo is a cutie, too."

Ryan parked the wagon, undid Dolly's harness, and put her in the small corral. Then Ryan put his arm out for Mary Elizabeth. When she tucked her arm into his, he patted it, and together they walked up to the door.

CHAPTER NINETEEN

MARY ELIZABETH WASN'T entirely sure she was ready for this. Dinner with strangers. Of course she had met Josiah and Jenna before. Josiah had actually asked her to supper once, but it was in the middle of his courtship with Jenna—although she didn't know that at the time—and they had probably just had a fight or something. But she had never actually had a real conversation with either of them, and so, they were strangers to her. Ryan's arm felt warm around hers, though, and she felt that if she was with him, she could face anything.

The door opened before Ryan had a chance to knock. Josiah stood there with a big grin on his face. "Come on in! Mary Elizabeth, Ryan. Good to see you both! Come in!"

Two dogs rushed out when the door opened, happy to be outside. Ryan waited until Mary Elizabeth had entered the house, and then he followed. Jenna, with an apron on, walked up to Ryan first and hugged him, and then hugged her. "Mary Elizabeth. So happy you could come and have dinner with us. Welcome to our home!"

She meant it. Mary Elizabeth felt strongly that she

really meant it. And for the first time in so many years, she felt that she was with people who really wanted her there. She couldn't remember when she last felt that way at home. It was certainly before moving out west. It was probably right around when she said no to Teddy Thornhill's proposal.

"Do you want to see Milo?" asked Jenna.

"Oh, the baby, yes!" Mary Elizabeth followed Jenna into a bedroom where the baby lay in a small crib, breathing silently and looking peaceful. "He's beautiful, Jenna. He's truly beautiful."

Josiah had followed them in, and now stood with his arm around Jenna. "We think so, yes."

Jenna burst out laughing, followed by Ryan and then Mary Elizabeth.

"What?" asked Josiah. "He is, isn't he? Beautiful, I mean."

"Come on, big guy," Jenna pulled Josiah out of the room. "Sometimes I find him in here with the baby," she said to Mary Elizabeth, "just staring at him and smiling. It's like he thinks that he created him all on his own."

Ryan howled with laughter, and Josiah said, "What?"

Mary Elizabeth just smiled and nodded her head. She wasn't used to people being this light-hearted. But she liked it.

"Jenna," Ryan said, "how soon is dinner?"

"Actually, Ryan, I'm a little behind. I'm sorry. I wasn't sure when you were coming, and I didn't want it to get cold."

"Would you guys mind if we took the horses out for a little spin around the block?"

"Spin around the block?" asked Josiah. "Ryan, you're doing it again," he said through slightly gritted teeth.

"Yeah, sure. Patches is already saddled."

"Mary Elizabeth? Are you game?"

She felt herself shrink back. "Oh, I don't know, Ryan. It's been so long since I've ridden."

"Oh, go ahead, Mary Elizabeth. Magic is a baby. And you'll remember how in no time. It's like riding a bicycle," said Jenna.

"Jenna!" said Josiah sternly.

Jenna waved her hand in the air. "Whatever!"

"Come on, Mary Elizabeth. You'll have fun." Ryan held his hand out to her.

She took his hand and followed him out of the house. The two dogs rushed up to them. Mary Elizabeth knelt down to pet them, and they licked her all over her face. "I love dogs!" When she stood up, the dogs pawed at the door, and Ryan opened it to let them in the house. Walking alongside Ryan, she said, "Ryan, I'm not sure about this at all. It's been so long."

"And you said you used to love it," he said, as he led her into the barn. "It will just take me a minute to saddle Magic, and we'll be ready to go. Do you want to help me brush him?"

Mary Elizabeth, having resigned herself to ride after all these years, decided that she might as well make the most of it. She took the brush from Ryan, and as she brushed Magic's black coat, she ran her hand along his back. He nickered at her.

"See? He likes you! You two will get along fine. You finished?"

"Yeah, he wasn't dirty at all. I just needed to get all the dust off."

After putting the saddle pad on, Ryan lifted the saddle onto Magic's back, Mary Elizabeth handed him the

85

cinch from the off side, and Ryan tightened it. "Can you remember how to put a bridle on?"

Mary Elizabeth reached out her hand to take the bridle from Ryan. "I think I can handle it!"

"Thata girl!"

Mary Elizabeth began to slip the bridle onto Magic's head. "Ryan? There's no bit on this bridle."

"It's called a hackamore, Mary Elizabeth. It works by putting pressure on the horse's nose. Jenna prefers it."

"Will I still be able to control him?"

"Shouldn't be a problem at all. You ready? You want me to give you a leg up?"

"Oh, sure. Thanks." Mary Elizabeth bent her leg, Ryan grabbed it and boosted her into the saddle. "I've never ridden in a regular skirt before, Ryan." She adjusted herself in the saddle.

"You okay?"

"So far, so good," said Mary Elizabeth. And as she sat in the saddle, the first time in so many years, it felt strangely familiar, and she realized how much she had missed it. And how glad she was that Ryan had talked her into this.

Ryan swung easily into the saddle and looked at her. "We'll just walk, if that's what you want." He led the way out of the barn and onto the main road.

She felt herself moving with the rhythm of the horse like she used to when she was a kid. Suddenly remembering how much she used to ride bareback, she asked, "Does Jenna ever ride him bareback?"

Ryan laughed. "Jenna *loves* riding bareback. Josiah practically had to tie her down to keep her from riding bareback when she was pregnant."

Mary Elizabeth nodded dreamily. "I used to ride like

that all the time. Old Cookie—who was young back then —and I used to ride like the wind. But after the long trip out here, and her getting older, all she can do is pull that wagon to town and back. I was actually glad when my father wouldn't let me use her to go to the next town. It was too much for her, but I didn't have the nerve to ask you if you had a wagon of your own."

Ryan put out a hand across the two horses and touched her arm. "Never be afraid of asking me any-thing, Mary Elizabeth. If it's in my power, I will do it for you."

She nodded and encouraged Magic to go a little faster. "Oh, it's been awhile since I've ridden a trot! Let's go!" She squeezed her legs, and Magic broke into a slow canter.

Ryan laughed and caught up. "You caught on pretty quick! I bet you could have ridden your father's stallion, after all!"

Mary Elizabeth turned to him, strands of her hair blowing out behind her. "I'm sure of it!" Leaning back in the saddle, she moved the reins slightly, and Magic slowed. "I think we ought to get back now; I should be helping Jenna."

Ryan smiled at her as they turned the horses around. "That's fine. I just wanted you to get a taste. Because I knew if you truly loved to ride, that it would only take a taste of it to get you back into it."

"You were right, Ryan." She looked at him with a serious expression. "I feel like you already know me better than most people do."

CHAPTER TWENTY

"PERFECT TIMING," SAID Josiah as they walked in the door.

"Jenna, can I do something to help?"

"Sure, put this on the table, will you?" She handed Mary Elizabeth a platter.

"Oh, smells good. What do you call this, Jenna?" She looked at the potatoes covered lightly with a crust of cheese.

"Um," Jenna looked at Josiah guiltily, "au gratin potatoes . . . ?"

"Oh, yes! I've had these before! And I loved them!"

"Phew!" said Jenna.

Josiah tried to look stern, although he was chuckling. And Ryan just watched the whole episode in amazement. He couldn't believe he was spending the afternoon with the woman of his dreams.

"Here, Mary Elizabeth. Can you put this on the table, too?"

Mary Elizabeth put the platter of meat on the table, and when Jenna showed her where the glasses were, she poured water from the pitcher into each of the glasses, and put them on the table.

"Let's eat!" announced Jenna, heading toward the table.

Jenna sat down, Josiah sat down, and Ryan helped Mary Elizabeth into her chair before sitting down across from her. "This all smells so good! Thank you so much for inviting me, Ryan, and thank you Jenna and Josiah for having me here. You make me feel like family." Mary Elizabeth looked down at her hands. "Well, better than family, actually."

"You're welcome, Mary Elizabeth," said Jenna, as she passed her the plate of lamb. "We're glad to have you."

"So you didn't accept the teaching job in the big city?" asked Josiah.

Mary Elizabeth shrugged. "I'm not a teacher, I didn't really want it. But it wasn't offered to me, anyway."

Ryan put his hand on her arm. "Mary Elizabeth, if you don't think it will bother you, go ahead and tell them the whole story. I know they'll agree with me. You know, *if* you're comfortable."

Mary Elizabeth told the whole story, and even though Ryan had heard it already, he paid rapt attention. When she finished, both Jenna and Josiah were nodding their heads.

"Oh, she definitely had it out for you!" said Jenna.

"And you can't blame her, Mary Elizabeth. You were more qualified than she was in her own position!" said Josiah.

"I told her that once a writer, always a writer, and that she shouldn't feel bad about that at all," said Ryan.

"Agreed," said Jenna and Josiah at the same time. When they said it together, they looked at each other and smiled, as Ryan watched. He loved how they were together, and he wanted that kind of relationship himself one day—he hoped with Mary Elizabeth.

"Tell them the rest, Mary Elizabeth. What happened on the stage," said Ryan excitedly.

Mary Elizabeth smiled at him and shrugged. "I started writing a novel on the way home. I wrote for the whole time, and now I have a bunch of pages!"

"Oh! That reminds me! I'll be right back!" Ryan jumped up from the table and ran out the front door.

Jenna stood up and started clearing the empty dishes off the table. Mary Elizabeth helped her carry everything into the kitchen. A minute later, Ryan returned carrying the saddlebag.

"What's that, Ryan?" asked Jenna.

"A present for Mary Elizabeth!" He stuck his hand into the saddlebag and pulled out a metal box.

"What is it?" asked Josiah.

"Wait a minute. I have to open it." Ryan fiddled with the locking mechanism until the cover came off, revealing a typewriter.

"A typewriter!" said Jenna. "A perfect gift for a writer!"

"What do I do with it?" asked Mary Elizabeth, confused.

"See the letters on the keys? Oh, wait." Ryan checked both sides of the saddlebag and pulled out his list of what he needed to buy from his last trip to town. He rolled the paper into the typewriter and with two fingers, typed out, "Hi there, Mary Elizabeth."

She gasped and said, "Let me try it! Let me try it!" She started looking at the keys and looked up at Ryan. "They're not in order."

"I'll get you a book on learning to type. You'll figure it out in no time!"

"Here, let me show you how it's done." Jenna stood by Mary Elizabeth, turned the typewriter, put all her fingers on it, and typed out, "You can write your whole novel on this." Then she turned the typewriter back toward Mary Elizabeth.

"That was so fast!" Mary Elizabeth put her fingers on the top row of keys. "How can you do it so fast?"

"Here," said Jenna, moving Mary Elizabeth's fingers to the second row. "You start here. That's called the 'home row.' But Ryan's right. You need a book, and then you'll learn how in no time."

Mary Elizabeth smiled at Ryan and then looked at Jenna. "Thank you, Jenna." Then, as if overcome, she stood up and turned away from them. "Where's the necessary?"

"Oh, it's, um, in that room. Go inside and turn right through the door. You'll see it."

Mary Elizabeth looked briefly up when Jenna said "in that room," and Ryan saw there were tears in her eyes. But she hurried into the room and closed the door behind her.

"Oh, Jenna," said Ryan, "you should have had her use the outhouse in the back."

"Nobody's been in that thing for a year, Ryan! I keep wanting Josiah to get rid of it, but he says we need it for show."

"Yeah, but nobody has an inside toilet yet. It's going to make her suspicious." Ryan stood up and began to pace nervously.

"I have an enlightened idea, Ryan. Let's tell her." Jenna put her hands on her hips and looked at him.

"Oh, no. That wouldn't be right. Not yet."

"Ryan, the sooner the better. I think Jenna's right.

91

Normally, I wouldn't say that, but I think Mary Elizabeth is up to it." Josiah walked over to stand in front of Ryan. "Let's tell her, man. It will be for the best. You'll see."

"I don't think it's a good idea at all, Josiah. I'm afraid I'll lose her."

Josiah looked at his friend and shook his head. "You might lose her if you don't. This is best. Be honest, Ryan."

Looking from Jenna to Josiah and seeing them so confident in their suggestion, Ryan said, "I'm afraid. I'm really afraid. Not yet. Let's not do it just yet."

CHAPTER TWENTY-ONE

IT WAS THE strangest thing. Whoever heard of a necessary *inside* a house? It seemed to work fine, although it
wasn't over a deep hole like regular necessaries. Perhaps
this was how they did it where they come from, thought
Mary Elizabeth. When she finished, she noticed there
was a pitcher and a bowl of water on the counter, and a
towel hanging above it. Not knowing if she should do
something with it or not, she poured the water over her
hands, and then wiped them with the towel. When she
stepped out of the small room, she heard Ryan's voice,
but it had an edge to it. What was he afraid of?

As she walked into the bedroom, she saw something
small in the window connected to some kind of wire.
What was that, she wondered. She had stopped the tears
from flowing when she entered the strange little room.
She couldn't believe how wonderful Ryan was to her—a
gift to help her with her writing! After composing herself
enough to return to the living room, she walked out
there confidently.

The typewriter was gone. It wasn't anywhere on the
table, and as she glanced around the room, it was

nowhere to be seen. "Where's my typewriter?"

"Um, I put it away. I didn't want it to bother you," said Ryan, looking down.

"Bother me? I love it! I couldn't believe that you would do that for me." She took a step forward and wanted to throw her arms around him, but didn't think it was appropriate.

"Oh, go ahead! Give him a hug! It's all right," said Jenna.

Mary Elizabeth laughed nervously and then threw her arms around Ryan. "Thank you, Ryan. Thank you for everything—including getting me back up on a horse." She looked into his eyes. "I think you're wonderful."

"Okay, you two, enough of that now. Let's go into the living room to talk." Jenna walked over there and sat next to Josiah on the couch.

Ryan and Mary Elizabeth sat on two chairs facing Josiah and Jenna. The dogs ran up to Mary Elizabeth, and she bent over to pet them. "What are their names? I really love dogs."

"The gray one is Jet, and the smaller one is Bingo," said Josiah.

Mary Elizabeth, petting each dog with one hand, looked up with a big smile on her face. "They're wonderful!" When the dogs wandered away, she sat back in her chair.

Ryan turned to her and smiled. "I'm so glad you like the typewriter, Mary Elizabeth. And I'll get you a book on typing, um, soon as I can."

"Now you can go home and type all you want!" said Jenna.

"Well, not exactly." Mary Elizabeth looked down and then back up at Jenna.

"Why not?"

"I didn't tell you about the quarrel with my parents. Briefly—after I told them about what happened and that I didn't want the job anyway, they were furious. My mother called me a spinster and ran from the room crying. And my father wanted me to apologize to *her*!" She shook her head. "You know, sometimes I think that I was born in the wrong time. There must be a time in the future where women can do what *they* want to do and not what their folks want them to do! Don't you think?"

The room stayed silent, but Mary Elizabeth thought that everyone's eyes had gotten big and that they looked at her with renewed interest. "And not only that," she continued, "but just to pile on the agony, my father wants to run me out of town on a rail unless I get a job! And when I told him there were no jobs in town, he said that since I'm a writer that I better start writing letters to find a job. He gave me two weeks." She shrugged. "So I'm kind of in a fix."

Josiah cleared his throat. "Um, Mary Elizabeth, we have something to tell you."

"No, Josiah, wait." Jenna put her hand on Josiah to stop him from speaking. "I have an idea for a job right here in town!"

"Really?" Mary Elizabeth's eyes were bright with interest. "Not the school teacher job, I hope!"

"No, Rachel's not leaving, and you wouldn't want that anyway! And this job wouldn't be exactly what you want, but you should have time to write while you're there! You know that Eliza and Samuel have gone East to find their son, right?" Jenna looked at Mary Elizabeth and waited for an answer. When she nodded, Jenna continued. "Granny and Edward are running the whole place and the restaurant, and frankly, although they haven't complained, it's too much for them. They could definitely use the help. And I could talk to them for you. What do you think?"

"Oh, Jenna, would you? Then I wouldn't have to absquatulate! It would be perfect until I figure out what I'm going to do about my parents, and by then, Eliza and Sam should be back."

"Oh, I don't think you'll have too long to wait to figure out what to do about your parents." Jenna stole a quick glance at Ryan and smiled, but Mary Elizabeth didn't understand what that would mean.

Josiah cleared his throat again. "Okay, finished?" he asked Jenna. "Now, Mary Elizabeth, we have something to tell you."

"Yes?" she asked.

CHAPTER TWENTY-TWO

"JOSIAH, LET RYAN do it," Jenna patted Josiah's arm again. "Ryan, you up for this?"

Ryan exhaled a long breath and then said, "If you really think I should."

"What?" asked Mary Elizabeth. "You all sound so serious. What do you have to tell me?"

"Wait. Wait. Before I tell her, what's absquatulate?"

"Leave. She won't have to leave. Now tell her, Ryan, tell her. Or I will." Josiah leaned forward on the couch until Jenna pushed him gently back with her arm.

Ryan faced her, and he looked tense. "It's what you said, Mary Elizabeth. You know, about another time where women can do what they want? It's not always true, though, some women—"

"Ryan! Get to the point!" said Josiah.

"Okay, okay. Sorry. There is a time like that, Mary Elizabeth. It's where we all came from."

"Where y'all came from? What do you mean? Jenna, Josiah, and you all came from where?"

"Not Josiah. But me and Jenna, Nick, Rachel, Granny, Sarah, and Kat. And it isn't *where* we came from as much

97

as *when* we came from."

"*When* you came from?" She shook her head. "I'm sorry, Ryan, I'm not following you." Mary Elizabeth glanced at Josiah and Jenna, but they both nodded toward Ryan to bring her attention back to him.

Ryan moved his chair so it was closer to hers. Then he picked up her hand. "May I hold your hand while I tell you this, Mary Elizabeth?"

She nodded. "Of course. But I still don't understand what you're trying to say to me."

"Mary Elizabeth, we are from the future—the future Red Bluff."

Mary Elizabeth took her hand from his and put both hands to her face as she doubled over with laughter. "Y'all," she motioned to all of them, "are trying to hornswoggle me! You had me there for a minute!" She looked at Ryan's, Jenna's, and Josiah's faces, and not one of them had even the hint of a smile. Sitting back in her chair, she said, "You're *not* trying to hornswoggle me?"

"I got caught in a spring snowstorm and stumbled onto a cave. When I came out the other side, it was here, in the nineteenth century."

"What century do you come from?"

"The twenty-first."

"That's impossible!"

Jenna leaned forward. "Do you remember why you told Josiah you didn't want to go out with him? It was because being a sheriff is a dangerous job, and you didn't want to be a widow. Right?"

"Yes, but you must not have been afraid of that."

"Of course I was afraid of that!" Jenna leaned back on the couch and snuggled into Josiah. "So I looked him up on something called the internet to find out when he died." She kissed Josiah on the cheek, and he smiled. "It's not anytime soon. And that's how I found out that Eliza and Samuel's son was still alive. I found the death record on one of her sons, but the other one didn't die until much later. And he died right here, in Red Bluff."

"But he's not *in* Red Bluff. I don't understand."

"He will be—as soon as Eliza and Samuel bring him home."

"But they thought he was dead, until you told them. That means—that means you were meant to tell them, so that he could come home!" She sat up and looked at them wide-eyed.

"Your girl catches on quick," said Josiah to Ryan.

"Maybe," said Jenna. "It's possible that he would have just come home on his own at some later time. We'll never know the answer to that question."

"And your necessary? Is that what they have in the future? Everybody has one *inside* their homes?"

"Yes, everybody has one inside, but they're much more advanced than that one. The new ones have water in them, and the waste just gets flushed away."

Mary Elizabeth shivered. "What else?"

Jenna walked into the bedroom and returned with the object that Mary Elizabeth had seen in the window, with the wire coming out of it. "See this? Here, put one of these in your ear." She handed her a set of in-ear buds that she had brought with her.

Mary Elizabeth looked at what Jenna handed her and then put it in her ear. "Oh! Music is coming out of this!" She jerked it out of her ear in surprise. "How does that work?"

Jenna held up the object that was attached to the other end of the iPod. "This is a solar charger. It creates power from the sun. Soon there will be electricity, and there will be electric lights in everybody's homes."

"I bet there's more, too, isn't there? More magical things?"

"Yes," said Ryan. "A lot more."

"With all these magical things, why would you want to leave there to come here?"

Jenna looked at Josiah with love. "I came for him."

"I came so I could paint. There wasn't enough time in the future. Here I have plenty of time," said Ryan.

"Sarah came because she wanted to sing, Kat came for Doc, Rachel came because she couldn't get a job, and Granny came because she fell in love with Edward," Jenna said. "We all came for a reason."

"And Nick came because he wanted to be deputy sheriff," said Josiah.

"Nick, too?" she asked.

They all nodded. Ryan moved in his seat uncomfortably. "Should we not have told you?" he asked.

At that moment, from the bedroom, the baby started crying. Jenna and Josiah both got up to take care of him. Mary Elizabeth heard Jenna say, "He's dirty, Josiah. Bring me a diaper. Then I'll feed him."

Mary Elizabeth stood up. "Ryan, I think I need to leave. If I don't get home soon, there will be more trouble." She stepped up to the bedroom door where Jenna and Josiah were. "Thanks so much for dinner! I enjoyed it very much! Good-bye!"

"Bye, Jenna, Josiah. Thanks, and I'll talk to you later." Ryan poked his head in and then walked to the front door. He opened it for Mary Elizabeth, and they walked outside into the sunshine.

CHAPTER TWENTY-THREE

MARY ELIZABETH WAITED in silence while Ryan hooked Dolly up to the wagon. When he helped her into the wagon, all she said was, "Thank you." They headed toward town.

Minutes and more minutes passed in silence. Soon they were more than halfway home, and still Mary Elizabeth hadn't said a word. Ryan was both horrified and terrified in equal measures. Horrified that in telling her about the future, he had ruined his chances with her, and terrified that he had lost her forever. Not that he ever had her exactly, but it felt like they were going in the right direction.

He didn't know what to do, and he didn't know what to say. Should he say something, or just leave her to her own thoughts? But after what he, Jenna, and Josiah had just told her, those thoughts could be anything. Saying something was probably better than the awful silence that hung between them.

"So, Mary Elizabeth, do you hate me now? Do you not want me to court you anymore?" he asked in a small voice.

She turned toward him, surprised. "Why would you think that, Ryan?"

"Because of what we told you—about where, I mean *when* we come from."

Reaching out, she placed her hand over his. "Ryan, the way you treat me—the way you look at me, I could *never* hate you. And of course I still want you to court me. Nothing has changed. It's just that—well, it's a lot to think about, you know? Another world out there, just like ours only nothing at all like ours. It's like a miracle. And a world where women don't have to be silent and do as they're told? It's just a lot to take in, that's all, Ryan. I'm a bit overwhelmed. Do you understand?"

He nodded. "I'm just glad you're not mad at me. They made me tell you, by the way. I thought it was too early."

"And what would you have waited for? For me to have already fallen madly in love with you? And *then* tell me? No, I think this was the right time. Thank you for telling me. Let me decide for myself."

"Okay," said Ryan, still feeling small. He wasn't sure they had done the right thing, but what had she said about falling in love with him? That excited him and scared him all at the same time. Had she really said that? Was she really falling in love with him? Or had the discussion about the future put a stop to that? Is that what she meant by deciding for herself? And the biggest question of all—was he falling in love with her? That thought scared him, too—probably more. Although he knew that he had never felt this way before, he had written it off to his lack of women for the past year. Or maybe that Mary Elizabeth was so different *because* she was from the nineteenth century. He had admitted to Nick that he was considering settling down, that much was true. But settling down and *love*—that was different. Love was very different.

Ryan sighed and relaxed some—not all the way, though, because it still felt strained between them. And now, he felt scared. Since he had never been in love before, had never even thought about being in love before, the idea of it made him feel skittish—like a horse ready to spook at the slightest disturbance. Was he ready to spook, run off, never return to this uneasy feeling? Or was he ready to confront it, embrace it, and enjoy everything that it had to offer? He shrugged; he wasn't sure. It could go either way—spook and run off or embrace it. And there was always the chance that she could spook and run—she said she hadn't decided yet. She may not hate him, but still she *could* think that it was all too much for her—a man from the future.

He sighed again as the silence closed in around them once more. There wasn't anything that he could do right now. Either the harm was done or the advantage was won. She did say that she hadn't decided yet. It could be that she liked the idea so much that she would even want to move there! Ryan smiled to himself at that thought, and gulped. Wait. He didn't want to move back to the new Red Bluff—he loved it here and wanted to stay. And what if she wanted to move to the future? What would he do then? It would almost be worse—he would have introduced her to it, and then lost her to it. Shaking his head almost imperceptibly because he didn't want her to see, he settled back into the movement of the wagon.

After a few more silent minutes, he made up his mind. "Mary Elizabeth, whatever you decide, know this. I *still* want to court you."

Mary Elizabeth nodded her head. "I've noticed that

you use some words that we don't use, and that we use some words that you're not familiar with. So language must have changed along with everything else. What do you call courting in your time."

"Well, it's not *my* time anymore. I want to stay here for the rest of my life. But it's called dating."

"Okay, Ryan Leyton. I would like very much to continue *dating* you." She patted his hand and smiled at him.

Ryan felt as though he would burst with joy. And an idea occurred to him that he hadn't thought of before. "Can I paint you?"

"Paint me? What do you mean?"

"You know, paint a picture of you. I'd love to paint a picture of you."

"You mean sit for you, model for you?"

"Yes, exactly! Would you?"

"Sure, tomorrow?"

"That would be great, Mary Elizabeth! That would be really, um, awesome!"

CHAPTER TWENTY-FOUR

MARY ELIZABETH WOKE up to a gloriously sunny day. At least *she* thought it was glorious. How could it not be after her wonderful afternoon the previous day? Dinner with Jenna and Josiah who treated her like family—no! They treated her better than family. That was for sure. And their "confession" about coming from the future! At first the whole thought of it was overwhelming—what a concept to grasp—but after using their inside necessary and then that object that played music! It had to be true. When she had thought about it the day before, when it was still fresh, she wondered what she should do about it. The idea of course had already started to take root in her mind, and now she knew exactly what she should do about it.

On the way home, Ryan had looked so nervous, not knowing how she took the incredible information. And she couldn't tell him yet what she was thinking, at least not until she was sure herself. Now she was sure, and she couldn't wait to tell him. The day before when he had dropped her off just down the street so her mother wouldn't see him, she had wanted so much to tell him what she was thinking. But it would be better now, when she was sure.

Since her mother was still not talking to her, she wasn't going to bother with breakfast. She just had to catch her father before he left for work, so he would leave her the wagon. But if he didn't, she smiled to herself, she had plans of her own. Quickly, she got dressed so she wouldn't miss him. When she heard him in the hallway, she opened her door and stepped out.

"Papa, could you please leave me the wagon today? I need to go into town."

"And what would you need to go into town for, I wonder? You have no job. We don't need any supplies. No, I think I will not leave you the wagon." He walked past her, then stopped and without turning around said, "Besides, you made it into town and back yesterday without any trouble."

Without answering, she walked back into her bedroom. So they knew. Fine. It didn't matter anyway. Now that she had the future as a possibility, she knew that she could just move there and not have to endure her mother calling her a spinster, and her father treating her like she was a nonentity. Knowing what she had to do, she searched in her chest of drawers to find what she was looking for. Going through the blankets and clothes quickly, she found it close to the bottom. Although she hadn't worn it since before she went to college, she had kept it—a split skirt her mother had made her for when she used to ride Old Cookie. Holding it up to her waist, she thought that it would still fit.

When she heard her father pull the wagon out of the yard, she slipped off the skirt she was wearing and slipped on the split skirt. It still fit her! A little snug at the waist, but otherwise a perfect fit. She waited five minutes for her father to disappear down the street before she quietly stepped out of her room and quietly closed the door behind her. Then she walked to the front door, opened it slowly so as not to make any sound, walked out, and closed it gently behind her.

Mary Elizabeth sneaked past the window where her mother may have been and walked out to the barn. Her father's red stallion, Rojo, a Spanish word meaning red, was in the stall at the far end of the barn. Cookie was always kept in the stall closest to the door so they were far apart. As she walked by Cookie's empty stall, she picked up the brushes that her father had left on the ground, and continued toward Rojo. When he saw her, he took a step back and showed her the whites of his eyes. She thought back and couldn't remember that she'd ever even touched him. He was her father's horse, and therefore not to be touched. Slowly, she stepped closer. Rojo jumped to the back of the stall and kicked out at the side wall with his hind feet.

"Easy, Rojo, easy boy." When she was a girl, she had watched many horse trainers. Some were mean, some were kind. The kind ones seemed to create better horses. Since she hadn't told Ryan what time she'd be there, she had plenty of time. "Come on, Rojo, we can do this, boy. You and I. We're going to be friends." Five minutes later, the big red horse allowed her to pet his nose. Slowly, she entered his stall and rubbed him on the neck. When she started scratching him, he stuck out his neck and made a funny face. "Gotcha now, Rojo!" She remembered hearing one of those trainers say that if you can find a horse's itchy spot, then you have found the way to their heart.

After brushing him down, she put the saddle pad and

the saddle on his back, and then cinched him up. When she went to put the bridle on him, he accepted it readily. Now, she was almost ready. Should she get on him in here and ride quickly past the window, or should she walk him outside giving her mother more time to see them? Better if she gets on in the barn. She checked the cinch again and climbed into the saddle. As soon as they were out of the barn and into the sunshine, Rojo reared straight up, standing on just his hind legs and whinnying loudly. Mary Elizabeth held onto Rojo's mane and leaned forward until the horse returned his front legs to the ground. She thought she saw her mother's shadow in the window. Oh, well, too late now. "Rojo!" she scolded. "Now you've really gotten me into trouble. You better be a good boy from now on and make it up to me."

When she rode into town, she was going to drop Rojo off at the livery, but the horse still felt so fresh that she felt guilty doing that to him. So she rode through town on the back street and when she reached the far edge of town, she encouraged Rojo to run. And he did! He ran like the wind! Her hair came undone, and it flowed out behind her like when she was a girl racing with Cookie. She was so grateful to Ryan for getting her back onto a horse. It had been so long that she had forgotten what an incredible, delicious pleasure it was.

CHAPTER TWENTY-FIVE

Ryan had everything ready. The chair—his most comfortable chair—sat in front of the split log interior of the store. His camera was set up on the tripod, and his computer on a table with a cover over it, in case someone came into the store who shouldn't see the out-of-place object. The camera could easily be explained. He didn't know if he'd scare Mary Elizabeth further with the camera and the computer, but he thought that he needed to use them. He didn't want her going through the boredom of sitting for him, if she was uncomfortable doing it. The camera and computer would solve that.

Since she hadn't said when she was coming, he wasn't worried about her being late. She would get there when she got there, and in the meantime, Ryan would restock some shelves and go through the coins in his cash box. Sitting down in the front of the store, he opened the cash box and began going through each coin. Almost immediately, he found one worth five thousand dollars. He stuck it in his pocket reserved for special coins. When he first started doing this, he would set them aside, and then absent-mindedly hand them to people for change. Luckily, one of the people was Josiah, who gave it back later. That's why he now had a special pocket reserved only for valuable coins. He found two more worth several hundred each that he also put in the special pocket.

When he heard the back door open, he was glad that he had covered the computer. As he stood up to see who had entered the back, Mary Elizabeth surprised him by strolling in from the back room.

"Hi, Ryan! I just had the greatest ride! Thank you again for getting me back on a horse!"

He smiled at her. "No problem. No problem at all. Who did you ride?"

"My father's stallion, Rojo. He gave me some trouble at first, then settled down."

"Does your father know?"

"Not yet! I don't know what he'll think when he finds out. But I don't care." She noticed he was going through the coins in his cash box. "Ryan, why do you do that? Look at all the coins with such interest?"

Ryan gave a quick glance around the store to make sure no one had sneaked in when he wasn't paying attention. "More future stuff, Mary Elizabeth. Some coins from the nineteenth century are very valuable in the twenty-first century." He reached into his pocket, pulled out the three coins, checked them quickly and handed her a nickel. "That one is worth five thousand dollars."

Mary Elizabeth looked at it incredulously. "Five thousand? It's a nickel!"

Ryan nodded. "I know!"

She handed the coin back to him and said, "Now something that my father told me several months ago makes sense. That boy, Zack. He used to come into the bank to look through coins. My father could never figure it out. This is why, isn't it?"

"Exactly! He found some really valuable coins that way. And his father, who had died years earlier, had coincidentally left him some coins, one of which was worth a million dollars! Zack and Madison are now living in style."

Her eyes drifted off into space as she continually nodded her head up and down. "I could do that, couldn't I? Make money that way?"

"Yeah, but what would your father think?"

"I'm really getting to where I don't care. Which is why I want to talk to you about something."

"Sure, but do you want to get started first? We can talk while you're doing the sitting."

"Back here?" She walked into the back room. "On that chair?"

"Yup, got it ready for you." When she sat down, Ryan asked, "Is it comfortable enough for you?"

"It's perfect, Ryan."

Ryan stood behind the tripod and started snapping pictures. "Hold perfectly still for just a minute."

When she saw him step away from the camera, she said, "What's that? I thought you were going to paint me."

"That's a camera—a twenty-first-century camera. Here, look at this." He put the memory card into the computer and the pictures popped up on the screen. "This is a computer. See your pictures? Now, if you get tired of sitting for me, I can refer to these, so I can paint the picture just right."

She smiled at him and shook her head. "It's like a miracle. But I don't mind sitting."

He set up his easel and began to paint. "You're so

beautiful," he murmured.

"Ryan?"

"Yes," he said, still concentrating on the painting.

"I'd like to go to the future with you."

"Sure, yeah." Then, realizing what she had just said, "What? You want to go there? What do you mean?" He put his brush down to look at her.

"I want to go, Ryan. I want to see all the miracles for myself. When can I go?"

"Oh, Mary Elizabeth, I thought you were thinking about it. I thought it overwhelmed you."

"It did, but this is what I want. I'm sure about it."

"If you're sure, then I'll take you this weekend during my regular supply run. Is that soon enough?" he asked, picking up his paint brush.

"I guess it will have to be. In the meantime, I'm going to spend some time at the bank. First thing I want to buy is my own horse! I don't know how far it is to the future, but I think it's too far for Old Cookie."

"You don't have to worry about your own horse, Mary Elizabeth. We'll take the wagon when we go, so I can bring supplies back."

"Yes, but if I have my own horse, I can return there on my own. Right?"

Ryan looked up, stunned. His first thought was, what have I done?

CHAPTER TWENTY-SIX

BEFORE RYAN COULD even begin to think of how to respond to that, Jenna walked in the store. "Ryan? You here?"

"In the back, Jenna!"

"Do you know where Mary Elizabeth is?" Jenna walked into the back room and saw Mary Elizabeth sitting there. "Oh! There you are! I just talked to Granny about a job, and she'd like to talk to you. Can you break away for a few minutes?"

Mary Elizabeth started to stand up, then looked at Ryan. "Can I?"

"Sure, yes of course! I can work from the photos."

She stood up and followed Jenna outside, where she was met by a wagging Jet. Kneeling down, she rubbed the dog's fur and got kisses in return. "I just love your dog! Thank you so much for doing this for me, Jenna. I can't tell you how much I appreciate it."

"No problem. No problem at all. This helps Granny and Edward out, too. The hotel and restaurant really are too much for them to run on their own. Besides, you'll get to know our grandmother by working there. I'll have to warn you, though. Granny can be really gruff. All you have to remember is that she's tough on the outside and warm and fuzzy on the inside. But she does call 'em like she sees 'em."

"She what?" asked Mary Elizabeth.

"Oh, sorry. It's a twentieth-century idiom that's not all that popular in the twenty-first century. But it seemed perfectly applicable to Granny."

"Do you mean she calls a spade a spade?" Mary Elizabeth looked at Jenna with upraised eyebrows.

"Yes! Exactly! You mean they even have clichés back in the nineteenth century? Oh, it probably isn't a cliché yet."

"What's a cliché?"

"Oh! Sorry! A cliché is a trite phrase. But as a writer friend said to me, there's a reason they're clichés! Anyway, now you know what I mean, and hopefully you'll know what to expect from Granny. Although, she constantly surprises all of us. Ah, here we are." Jenna opened the door of the hotel and let Mary Elizabeth enter first.

Granny stood behind the front desk going through papers, but turned around when she heard them come through the door. "Hi again, Jenna. Hello, Mary Elizabeth. I remember seeing you a year ago when I first moved to town. Didn't you and your family live here at the hotel for a while?"

"Yes, that's right, Mrs. Um?"

"Oh, not Mrs. Um, you can just call me Granny. Everybody else does, except those who call me worse."

Mary Elizabeth stifled a laugh. "Okay, Granny."

"And your father—isn't he that grump over at the bank?"

114

This time, Mary Elizabeth couldn't stifle her laughter. "Yes," she giggled, "that's exactly him."

"So I hear you're looking for a job?"

"Yes, my father—the grump—basically told me to find a job or he'd ride me out of town on a rail."

Granny shook her head and frowned. "Sounds like your father is worse than just a grump, but I'll keep that to myself. Okay, then." Suddenly, she looked at Jenna. "So where's that great-grandson of mine?"

"Josiah has him. That man just can't get enough of that baby!"

"Well, go get him! I need to see my great-grandson!"

"Okay, Granny, okay! I'll go get him. I wouldn't want to disappoint you!" Jenna hurried toward the hotel door.

"Just take your time, Granddaughter." As Jenna slipped out the door, Granny said, "Talking about the particulars of a job should be between you and me. If Jenna is as smart as I think she is, she'll stay away for a while. Now where were we? Oh, yes, your father was going to run you out of town on a rail, the jerk. So, I'll tell you, Mary Elizabeth, we really need someone here to help. And since you really need to get out of the house, I'm going to take advantage of you."

Mary Elizabeth smiled. "Okay."

"I'd need you here first thing in the morning, say eight o'clock, for the check-outs and to help in the restaurant if we get busy. I'd need you here from eleven to one-ish," Granny moved her head from side to side, "to help with lunch, I mean dinner—if we're busy—if not, you're free. And lastly, I'd need you in the late afternoon for check-ins and to help out for supper at the restaurant. The times in between—unless I ask you to stay—are your own. You can bring your typewriter here and write—I still can't believe that grandson of mine gave you a type-writer—or you can even go to the store and spend that time with Ryan. Your choice."

"Granny? Could I spend that time at the bank?"

"At the bank?" Granny raised her voice and drew back her head, looking at Mary Elizabeth like she was crazy. "Why would you want to spend time at the bank with that jerk of a father of yours?"

Mary Elizabeth laughed again. "I don't want to spend it with him, I want to spend it looking through coins."

Granny nodded. "Looking through coins, huh? So my silly grandson didn't just give you a typewriter, he also told you where—or *when*—we're from, huh? I honestly didn't think he was that much of an idiot."

"Actually, it was Jenna and Josiah that made him do it. He didn't want to."

"Well, that makes me feel better about him, then. But it wasn't any of their business, really. What do you think about that information? Are you going to dump my grandson now?" Granny looked at her defiantly.

"Dump?"

"Old woman," said Edward, striding up to the front desk, "let me help you out here. What my bride would like to know, Mary Elizabeth, is if you're going to give Ryan the mitten?"

"Oh! No! Definitely no! I already asked him to—you know—take me there."

"She wants to see the elephant, of course," said Edward.

"What elephant?" asked Granny.

Edward walked behind the counter and grabbed Granny around the neck, pretending to choke her. "Old woman! Stop acting daft! You know perfectly well what elephant!"

Granny cackled with pleasure as Edward hugged her. She looked up at him with love in her eyes. "I dearly love to tease that man." Then she looked at Mary Elizabeth again. "Now back to business. During the time that you're not required to be here, you can write, you can visit my grandson or anybody else, you can go home, and you can even spend time with that jerk of a father of yours looking at coins. Understood?"

Mary Elizabeth nodded. "Understood. It sounds perfect. When would you like me to start?"

"We're having several people coming in tonight and staying for two or three days. I assume they'll be eating all their meals here. If you can start tomorrow, that would be great. You didn't ask what I was going to pay you, though," said Granny.

"If the coin trick works out, it won't matter, right?"

Granny smiled and nodded. "No wonder your father wants to run you out of town. You're too smart for your own good. I was going to say fifty cents a day—of course, if you were a man, it would be a dollar. But since you don't care, how about a penny a day?"

Mary Elizabeth stepped back, surprised. "Really? That's all?"

"The penny or the fifty cents? I assume you mean the penny, because the fifty cents is pretty standard, um, this year. Let's do it this way, Mary Elizabeth. After you find your coins and go to *town*, you let me know if you want fifty cents a day or a penny a day. But let me give you a hint. Ask Ryan for a copy of Zack's list of valuable coins. There's one here somewhere," Granny started going through the papers again, "but I don't know where it is, and I don't care, anyway. I live here and now. And Edward and I have plenty of money for our life *here*. We don't need anything but each other. Right, dear?"

Edward had wandered away and now called out from the other room, "Anything you say, dear!"

Granny put out her hand and looked at Mary Elizabeth. "Deal?"

"Deal," Mary Elizabeth said, shaking Granny's hand.

CHAPTER TWENTY-SEVEN

MARY ELIZABETH WALKED out into the sunshine and looked around at the dirt road and the buildings. She wondered how different the Red Bluff of the twenty-first century would be. Would the roads be wider or narrower? Would the wagons be bigger or smaller? Surely people still rode horses, because everyone who moved here had a horse. But with the indoor necessary and that miraculous object that played music, there certainly had to be many changes. She could hardly wait!

After crossing the street, she continued walking toward Ryan's store. She glanced in the window at the sheriff's office and saw Josiah with one arm around Jenna and the other arm holding the baby. They looked so happy and acted so happy together! Would she ever have that kind of happiness? Could she and Ryan have that kind of happiness *together*? Although she didn't know the answer to that question, she did know that she enjoyed every minute that she spent with him now.

"Hi, Ryan!" she called, as she walked into the store.

No one else was in there, and she was glad. When he walked out from the back room, he had a big grin on his face like he was really happy to see her. "Did you get the job?" he asked.

"Yes! And it's perfect! It sounds like I will have plenty of time to write and go to the bank."

"Go to the bank? Why? To see your father?"

"Ugh, no. For the coins! Granny suggested that I ask you for a copy of the coin list that Zack gave you."

Ryan rummaged behind the counter, brought up a sheet of paper, and held it up for her to see. "I'll make a copy of it, but there's a book you should look at as well."

"Can I just borrow the list for now and look at the book later? I want to go to the bank now and look at some coins."

"Sure, here it is. It's pretty self-explanatory: the type of coin, nickel, dime, whatever, then the year and mint mark, O or S or P, and its possible worth on the end. The better condition it's in, the more it's worth." He handed her the list. "Do you have any money or do you need some?"

"I still have money left over from my trip."

"Don't spend any gold dollar pieces. They're often worth more."

"Okay. Thanks, Ryan! See ya soon?"

"I'll be here," said Ryan, "waiting to see your pretty face again!"

Mary Elizabeth smiled at him and walked out of the store with the paper in her hands. She didn't know how her father would react to her at the bank, but she was about to find out. After entering the bank, she walked up to the teller. "Hallo, Mr. Smythe."

"Hallo, Mary Elizabeth. Are you looking for your father?"

"No, I'd like to buy some coins, please." She pulled

out a bunch of coins, leaving the two gold pieces behind. When she counted it out, she had fifteen dollars and forty-two cents. "Can I have fifteen dollars in gold pieces, please?"

Mr. Smythe shrugged. "Sure, Mary Elizabeth." He counted out money from his drawer. "Here ya go." He handed her the fifteen gold pieces.

"Is it okay if I go in there to look at them?" she asked, pointing to the back room.

"Yes, of course, Mary Elizabeth. No one is in there."

"Thanks!" She walked back there, sat at the table, read quickly over the sheet of paper, and laid out the coins in front of her—face up so she could see the date.

Before she even had time to look at the date on the first coin, her father burst into the room. "What are you doing here?" he demanded.

Mary Elizabeth was not going to get caught up in his anger. "I'm just here to look at some coins. I won't bother you."

"What's this?" He snatched at the piece of paper before she had a chance to hide it. "What is this? How many of each were minted? Some of these numbers seem wrong. What do you need to do this for, anyway? Why aren't you out writing letters to find yourself a job?" He dropped the paper back on the table with disinterest.

"I'm doing it because I want to. And I've found a job. I start tomorrow. So I'll need to use the wagon, please."

"You found a job? What do you mean you found a job?"

"I—found—a—job. That's what I mean."

"Where?" he raised his voice. "Where could you possibly find a job around here?"

"The hotel. Now do you mind if I get back to what

121

I'm doing? I'd like to be getting home soon."

"How did you get to town, anyway?"

She looked at him. Should she tell him that she rode his fancy red stallion into town? No. "How do you think," she said it not as a question.

"Well, if you walked here today, then you can walk here tomorrow. I need the wagon myself."

"Fine," she said and picked up the first coin, ignoring him.

Exasperated at her lack of response, her father stormed out of the room. Mary Elizabeth checked the list and the first coin wasn't on it. Neither was the second, third, or fourth. The fifth coin was on the list, and if she read it right, it was quite valuable. She quickly checked the two gold pieces in her handbag—neither of them were on the list—kept one out and slipped in the valuable one she had found. None of the other coins was on the list. She glanced at the list of coins one last time, and noticed all the ten dollar gold pieces on the list. Until she came up with a solution, she had thought that she didn't have enough money with her to look at any.

Walking back up to the teller window, she set her coins aside, and said, "Mr. Smythe, can I just see a ten dollar gold piece, please?" She looked at the date and handed it back to him. "A different one, please?" With the second one, she struck gold. Handing him ten of the dollars that she had already looked at, she said, "Thank you!" and walked out of the bank and across the street.

"Ryan! Ryan!" she called out as she entered the store. "Look what I found!" She dug into the bottom of her purse and pulled out the two coins. If I read the list right, I think they're both worth a thousand dollars!" She handed him the coins and the list. "Would you keep the coins for me until we go? I don't trust my father."

"Sure, Mary Elizabeth, of course." Ryan smiled without looking at the coins in his hand. "I'll make you a copy of this list." He held up the paper. "When do you want to look at the coin book?"

"I start work tomorrow, but I should have some time during the day. How about then?"

"Perfect. Do you want to sit for me awhile longer?"

"Sorry, Ryan. I really ought to be getting home."

"That's fine. I'll see you tomorrow then?"

"Sure! Thank you for the list and the help and everything. See you tomorrow!" She smiled warmly at him and walked out the front door. After picking up Rojo at the livery, she rode him home, unsaddled him, brushed him thoroughly, and then walked into the house and into her room.

It wasn't long before she heard her father outside parking the wagon and putting Old Cookie into the barn. And it wasn't much longer after he walked inside and talked to her mother that he pounded on her bedroom door and stormed in before Mary Elizabeth had a chance to say, "Come in."

"What do you mean by riding my horse? You could have been killed!"

"Rojo was fine. He didn't complain."

"That's *my* horse! *You* can't ride him!"

"Cookie is *my* horse, and yet you harness her to the wagon every day and take her. Why don't you harness Rojo?"

"That's preposterous, and you know it's preposterous. I forbid you to ride my horse anymore!"

"Then leave me the wagon, and I won't have to."

Without even answering, her father stepped out of the

123

room, slamming the door behind him.

CHAPTER TWENTY-EIGHT

AFTER MARY ELIZABETH left, Ryan unconsciously started to put the two coins in his "safe" pocket, but stopped himself at the last minute. He had already put coins in there and didn't want to mix up hers with his. Glancing down at the coins and then checking Zack's list, he was pleasantly surprised. The first coin, a gold dollar, was from 1863 and worth about $1600. The second one, a ten dollar gold piece was an 1870 CC. The 1870 S was worth $1200, but the CC was worth nearly twenty thousand dollars! Mary Elizabeth had struck it rich on her first try, and she didn't even know it! She wasn't even gone more than half an hour, and she made a fortune! Wait till she finds out! He could hardly wait to see her the following day and tell her the great news. Now that he knew which coins they were, he slipped them into his pocket and returned to his painting.

It was coming along, but it would be better if she could sit for him again. Although he could use the photographs that he took of her to help him along, he wasn't ready to do that. He needed the live model. He needed her—Mary Elizabeth. And he didn't just need her for the painting. It was finally beginning to get through his thick skull that he needed a woman like her in his life. Ryan needed *her* in his life. And as long as she was willing, that was exactly what he was going to do. Maybe he'd say something over the weekend, when they traveled to the new Red Bluff together. Or maybe he'd wait until the trip back, when she'd be thrilled with what she had seen there. That might be a good time to approach her.

Someone came in the front door of the store and required Ryan's help. When they left, someone else came in, and Ryan got to talking, and then someone else and someone else, and soon the afternoon was gone. He put away his paints that he hadn't even gotten to all afternoon, cleaned his brushes, locked the front door, and walked upstairs to his apartment to make supper.

If there was one thing that he missed in the nineteenth century, it was TV dinners or frozen leftovers and a microwave oven. Sometimes he even thought that he wouldn't mind living in the new Red Bluff again. Life certainly was easier there. But then, he'd look around at the blue sky and the store that allowed him time to paint, and he would realize that this—the nineteenth century— was truly his home after all.

After starting a fire in his wood cooking stove, while he waited for it to get hot, he cut up mushrooms and a cucumber. Then he put a large pan filled with water onto the stove. When it started boiling, he added the spaghetti noodles, and put some tomato sauce, cut up mushrooms, and a cucumber in another pan, and placed it on the heat. When the noodles got al dente, he took the pan off the heat, poured out the water, and poured the tomato sauce mixture into the pan. Stirring it all around, he plopped some on a plate and ate until he was full. He put the remainder into a glass container and placed it into a small battery operated refrigerator. He didn't keep anything hidden in his apartment. Aside from Jenna, Nick, and Josiah, no one had ever been up there.

After dinner, he lit a candle and placed it close enough to the window that people could see it flickering. Then he sat in his easy chair and turned the switch on the bright battery operated lantern. Pulling his iPad out of a drawer, he played computer games until the battery ran out. Now he couldn't use it again until the sun did its job and recharged the battery. Pulling out the book he had been reading, he read until his eyes felt so tired that he couldn't read anymore.

He fell asleep about five minutes after his head hit the pillow. Awaking with a start, he stood up to look out the window. No snow. There was a dream that was quickly fading from his memory—something about snow and Mary Elizabeth. Disturbed by it, he couldn't fall back to sleep for hours. When he woke up the next morning, the sun was already bright in the sky, and someone was knocking loudly on the front door.

His first thought was that it was Mary Elizabeth. She had said she'd be by today. But after racing downstairs expectantly, he found that it was just Rachel, needing some last minute school supplies. Disappointed, Ryan watched her move around the store picking up several items. Then she paid and quickly left without saying more than two words. Leaving the door unlocked, he walked back upstairs to make some coffee and eat a sweet roll. He didn't know when Mary Elizabeth would show up, but he couldn't wait. Her presence in his life had become a joyful necessity instead of just pleasant female companionship.

CHAPTER TWENTY-NINE

EARLY THE NEXT morning, Mary Elizabeth, her stomach growling because she hadn't eaten the day before, got dressed and waited impatiently to see if her father was going to leave her the wagon. She felt grateful that he left earlier than usual and rode his stallion, Rojo. The wagon was hers! She ran outside and inhaled the fresh air. Stuck in her room for too long because she wouldn't eat with her annoying parents, she was ready to get out of the house. She brushed and harnessed Old Cookie, drove the wagon to town, and dropped it off at the livery.

Racing into the hotel, she looked around for Granny, and found her in the restaurant. "Hi, Granny!"

"You're here early today, Mary Elizabeth."

"I'm hungry. Do you think I could get something to eat before I start?"

"Of course, girl! Come on in, you do look famished. Isn't that jerk of a father feeding you?"

"My mother still isn't talking to me, so I haven't been eating at home."

"Sit down here, and I'll bring you a good meal!" Granny hurried into the back, and five minutes later came out with a plateful of eggs, ham, and toast, and set it in front of Mary Elizabeth.

"Oh, my goodness, Granny, this is too much food! I won't be able to get into my dress tomorrow!"

Granny came over and patted her shoulder. "I have a feeling you need it. And it's not your dress that's the problem." She leaned over and whispered into Mary Elizabeth's ear. "I'll tell you a secret. Nobody from the *new* Red Bluff wears a corset." Granny straightened up and winked at her.

Mary Elizabeth, shocked, said, "You're kidding."

Granny shook her head and smiled. "No. I'm not." Then she walked away.

The meal was delicious, but before Mary Elizabeth had a chance to finish, she heard loud talking and a clatter on the stairs. Then six men tramped into the restaurant and sat down at two tables.

Mary Elizabeth immediately stood up, picked up her plate, and carried it into the back kitchen area. Looking around for Granny and seeing her washing dishes, she said, "Granny, a bunch of people just walked in. What do you want me to do?"

Granny glanced at the plate of food, not yet finished, and smiled at her. "I think you're going to work out fine here, Mary Elizabeth. In the new Red Bluff, you know what we call what you just did? We call it being proactive. You didn't wait for me to ask you to help, you came in here to ask what to do. I think I'm going to like you. In fact, I like you already!" With her hand still drip-ping with water, she pointed to where the menus were. "Give each of them one of those and a glass of water. The glasses and pitcher are over there." Nodding toward another counter, she said, "When they're ready, take their order with the pencil and paper over there. And thank you!"

Mary Elizabeth grabbed the menus and hurried out. After handing one to each person, she returned to the kitchen, poured the water, put the glasses on a platter that she found in the same place, carried them out, and distributed them.

As she walked back into the kitchen, Granny handed her the pencil and paper. "Give them enough time to decide, but not too much time. If they ask you for more time, that's fine, but don't keep them waiting if they're ready."

"How can I tell?"

"Experience. Until then, you stay where they can see you. But don't just stand there—wipe off tables or something. Just be—available. Now go take a look at the tables. If they've closed the menus, then they're ready. If they're still pointing to items and talking among themselves, then they're probably not."

Mary Elizabeth peeked out and saw that they were still looking at the menus. "Still looking," she said to Granny.

"Give them another minute and then walk out."

Mary Elizabeth nodded, waited a minute, and then approached one of the two tables. She wrote everything down and brought the information back to Granny.

"Thank you. I'll prepare all this. I think it's too much for you to learn to cook, too, today. But if this group stays any longer, you'll have to!"

After Mary Elizabeth served the group, cleaned up after they left, and washed the dishes, Granny said she wanted her to learn procedures at the front desk. They had just gotten started when John Mills poked his head in the door. Granny elbowed Mary Elizabeth, and she looked up.

"Can I help you, Sir?" asked Granny politely.

"Um, yes, Mary Elizabeth told me that she was working here, I just wanted to be sure that she really was. I see that she's here." He stepped through the doorway and nodded toward Mary Elizabeth.

Granny elbowed Mary Elizabeth gently so her father couldn't see, and then she said, "Oh. Is Mary Elizabeth a liar, then? Perhaps I should have considered that before I hired her." It was all Mary Elizabeth could do to keep from laughing out loud. Even if Granny hadn't elbowed her, she realized that Granny was just playing John Mills.

"Um, no. Not usually. But, er, well, I just wanted to be sure."

"Well, Mr. Mills, she's doing a right bang-up job!" Granny smiled at him and patted Mary Elizabeth on the shoulder.

She had never seen her father so bewildered in his life. But as she got to know Granny better, she thought that the old woman could do that to anybody.

He grabbed the door and opened it. "Well, I guess that's good then. See you at home, Mary Elizabeth! Good-bye!" And he scurried out the door.

Granny chuckled and said, "That is how you handle a man like that, Mary Elizabeth. You turn the tables on him so he is on the defensive and not the offensive. It works every time! Well—almost every time."

They returned to the front desk procedures, and by the time they finished, it was time for dinner, and the group returned. The whole day sped by, and Mary Elizabeth didn't have time to leave the hotel. At the end of the day, Granny told her she had done a great job and

131

then insisted on feeding her supper. When she finally left the hotel, it was almost candle-lighting, but she needed to see Ryan.

She hurried up the street and walked into the store. Ryan was pacing back and forth behind the counter. "Hi, Ryan."

"Mary Elizabeth! I was so worried, but I was busy all day and couldn't go check on you!"

"I was busy all day, too, and this was the first chance I had to stop by. Will you walk with me to the livery? I don't want to go home in the dark, so I have to hurry."

"Sure, let's go." He led her out through the back door. "Listen, in case you're too busy the next few days, let's arrange now for this weekend. Can you meet me here at nine o'clock, or would you prefer that I pick you up?"

Mary Elizabeth thought for a moment and said, "I'll meet you at the store. I'm really excited about going!"

When they reached the livery, they found that Ezra had the wagon waiting for her. "Thanks, Ezra!" Ryan helped her into the wagon. "I'll see you Sunday if not before, Ryan!"

CHAPTER THIRTY

IT HAD BEEN days since Ryan had seen Mary Elizabeth. And finally, this day had come—the day they were to travel together to the new Red Bluff. He couldn't wait to see what she thought of the future that he had come from. And he really hoped that she liked it—but not *too much*. The way he felt about her—the longing—was getting worse the more days that he didn't see her. On their way home today, he would definitely have to mention it to her.

At eight o'clock, Mary Elizabeth walked in through the front door. Surprised, he looked up with a smile. "I didn't expect to see you this early!" Treading quickly across the floor, he grabbed her up in his arms and swung her around. When he saw the astonishment on her face, he put her down and said, "Oh, sorry! It's just that I haven't seen you in so long! But I didn't expect you so early."

"I had to come early so my father would think I was working. Yesterday when I harnessed Old Cookie, he came out and questioned me about where I was going. I told him truthfully that I was working. Today, he didn't ask, thankfully, or I'd be walking."

"Since you're so early, would you mind sitting for me again? I haven't done much on your painting since you were last here."

"No, I don't mind, but do you have anything to eat? I'm starved! Sorry, but I don't eat with my folks anymore, because my mother isn't talking to me."

Ryan looked at his watch. He kept a wind-up pocket watch now to fit in with the times. "You know, if we leave right now, we might catch Madison and Zack just as they're eating breakfast. Then you can get to know them. And if we miss them, then I can take you out. How does that sound?"

"Perfect! Let's go!" She held out her arm to him, and they walked to the back door of the store. He opened the door for her, she walked outside, and he followed. "Oh, Ryan, I'm so excited!"

"I hope you're not disappointed. Right here in the nineteenth century is a much better place."

"I won't be disappointed! I just know it!"

When they reached the livery, he said, "Mary Elizabeth, would you mind brushing Dolly? She's right down there. I'll get the wagon ready."

"Sure!"

Ryan had the wagon prepared when Mary Elizabeth led Dolly outside. He harnessed Dolly, helped Mary Elizabeth into the wagon, and they were off. Reaching over, he squeezed her hand. "I'm glad you're so excited. We'll have a good time."

When Ryan turned off onto the side trail, Mary Elizabeth frowned. "I've seen this trail before, but never tried it. Aren't you afraid that the wrong someone will follow it into the cave?"

"Are you thinking about what happened to Sarah? The men who kidnapped her?" Although they had never spoken about it, the whole town knew about the kidnapping.

"Yes, that would have been terrible—those awful men in the twenty-first century."

"You're right about that. Doc thought the trail on the other side of the cave was too apparent, so he and Zack camouflaged it. I suppose we should do the same thing here."

"What's camouflage?"

"Oh! I didn't realize that was a new word, sorry. It means disguising it so it blends in with the surroundings." They had come to the cave. "Are you ready?"

"Yes . . . no . . . maybe! Does it hurt when you get to the other time?"

"No, you won't feel it at all. The cave is short, and we'll be there in a minute. Here we go!"

Mary Elizabeth brought both hands to her face and covered her mouth. They entered the cave, she glanced around briefly, and then they were on the other side. Blue sky greeted them when they emerged. "Are we there?"

"Yep, this is it."

"It's not cloudy like it is in the old Red Bluff."

"I know. The weather isn't always the same. When Jenna got caught in the snowstorm that day, it wasn't snowing at all in the nineteenth century."

"It doesn't look any different here."

"No, not yet, but it will."

Just then, a jet roared overhead. "What's that?" Mary Elizabeth cowered down in the seat next to him.

135

"It's okay, it's okay. Don't worry. That's called a jet. They have lots of flying machines here. That's one big difference."

"Do they ever fall down?"

"Once in a great while, but everyone says that they're safer than cars."

"What are cars?"

He patted her hand. "You'll find out soon enough. We'll take my car where we have to go today."

She was silent as they went over the bumpy path to the main trail, occasionally glancing upwards where the jet had passed. And she stayed silent all the way to the gates that led to Jenna's house where Zack and Madison lived. Every once in a while, he would pat her hand, and she would give him an uncomfortable smile. "I didn't realize I would be this skeery. Is this it?"

"Yeah. Can you drive the wagon while I open and close the gates?"

She took the reins from him and looked uncomfortable as he worked the gates. Then he climbed back up and drove them to where he parked the wagon. He took Dolly out of the harness and turned her loose in the pasture, while Mary Elizabeth stood by, her back to the wagon and looking around skeptically. Ryan took her hand gently. "You ready?"

"I guess so. I'm feeling all-overish."

"Don't be afraid. I'm here with you. Okay?"

She nodded.

CHAPTER THIRTY-ONE

TRUTH WAS, SHE was terrified. That jet flying in the sky! That did it. Mary Elizabeth had expected differences, but large pieces of machinery flying through the air like a bird? It was just too much. Now she was afraid of what other skeery things she might find. Although she was clutching his hand tight enough to break bones, or at least it felt that way to her, Ryan smiled at her comfortingly.

They walked through the barn and out onto something that wasn't dirt or stone. Looking down, she stamped her foot and was surprised to find out how firm it was. "What is this, Ryan?"

"It's called cement. You won't find much dirt or grass in the city. We're lucky to be at the edge out here where we have the pastures."

When she looked up, she noticed them, and her eyes widened. "What are *those*?"

Ryan smiled. "Those, my dear, are cars. Are you ready to take a ride in one?"

Mary Elizabeth shook her head. "Not really. Do we have to?"

"We don't have to yet. Let's hope that Zack and Madison are up already. If not, we'll take the car to a restaurant."

"I hope they're up," she said.

The house was large—easily as big as their home in Atlanta, but it was all one story. And it appeared that much of the property surrounding it also belonged to the house. She wondered if all the twenty-first-century people lived like this.

Ryan knocked on the door and called out, "You guys up yet? Visitors!"

When Zack opened the door, Ryan said, "Glad to see you dressed, Zack! You know Mary Elizabeth, don't you?"

"Sure. Hello, Mary Elizabeth! Come on in! We're just making breakfast. Would you like to join us?"

"Hi, Zack. Sure! I'm starved."

She felt good that it was Zack who opened the door. The sight of him, who she had seen so many times before in the old Red Bluff, comforted her and made her feel more at home. Still unsure of herself, she waited for Ryan to go through the door first, and she followed him inside. They walked into a living room, and Ryan turned to her.

"Do you want me to explain all of this stuff," he waved his arm around the room, "now, or after breakfast?"

"Definitely after breakfast! I'm so hungry."

Zack, who had walked on ahead, said, "We have it almost all ready. Come on in. Mary Elizabeth, do you know Madison?"

Mary Elizabeth walked into the kitchen, looked at the young woman, and smiled. "Hi, Madison!" She had seen her in town a few times before, but they had never spoken.

"Hello, Mary Elizabeth! Welcome to the twenty-first century!" she said with a big smile on her face. "Please sit down and make yourself at home. Mi casa es su casa. Oh, sorry, I mean—"

"Gracias." Mary Elizabeth sat down and smiled at Madison's shock.

"She went to college," said Ryan, sitting down beside Mary Elizabeth.

"And I took Spanish there," said Mary Elizabeth. "Mostly everyone took French, but I chose Spanish to be different."

"You went to college?" asked Zack, surprised. "In the nineteenth century?"

"Her father is a banker, Zack. They have money. And money makes as much of a difference there as it does here." Ryan looked at Mary Elizabeth and patted her hand.

"Enough talk. Let's eat!" Madison put a plate in front of Mary Elizabeth, who just looked at it, blankly. "Is something wrong? Don't you like eggs?"

"It looks exactly like what I've been eating for breakfast all week," said Mary Elizabeth. "I expected food to be as different as everything else." Still starving, she picked up her fork and dived into the eggs and bacon.

"Bet you haven't had this, though." Madison put a glass of orange juice next to Mary Elizabeth, who took a hesitant sip.

"Yes! But I haven't had it since I left Atlanta." She finished the juice in just a few sips. "I've missed it!"

Madison poured more juice into her glass. "Have as much as you want. Ryan, why don't you 'import' orange juice like you 'import' salad?"

"I never thought of it. But how could I keep it cold? How would anyone keep it cold? But I could 'import' oranges."

"Oh, would you, Ryan?" asked Mary Elizabeth, her hand covering her egg-filled mouth. "I love oranges!"

Ryan looked at her with what she thought was love in his eyes. At least she hoped it was love in his eyes, because more and more she was beginning to realize that what she felt for him was love. "Of course, dear." He looked at Zack and Madison. "Mary Elizabeth and I had dinner over at Josiah and Jenna's house."

"They have a really nice place, don't they?" asked Madison.

"Very nice. And I just *love* their dogs! I've always wanted a dog, and my father would never let me have one. He said a horse was enough and that a dog wasn't practical."

"Your dad sounds mean," said Madison. "Did you want any more eggs? Bacon?"

"No thank-you. Granny just calls him a jerk!"

"That sounds like Granny!" Madison put the last of the eggs and bacon onto Zack's plate.

"Hey, Zack. You'll never guess what Mary Elizabeth found! Take a look at this." Ryan reached into his pocket, pulled out the saved coins, picked out the ten dollar gold piece, and handed it to Zack.

When Zack looked at it, he gasped. "Wow! Mary Elizabeth, this is an awesome find! It's worth thousands!"

Mary Elizabeth gave Ryan a sly look. "Did you switch coins on me so it would be worth more? Because I thought it was only worth a thousand."

Before Ryan had a chance to answer, Zack said, "Oh,

you probably got it mixed up with the 1870 S, which is worth a thousand. But this one is an 1870 CC, see?" he held it up for her to see. "It's an easy mistake, but the difference between the two coins is nearly twenty thousand dollars!"

"Really? It's worth that much? Wow! I can buy my own horse now!"

"You can buy a horse and a computer and—" Zack flipped the coin over to see the back.

"A computer?" asked Mary Elizabeth.

"You know, remember the computer I showed you at the store? I put the pictures that I took of you on it."

"Oh, yeah, a computer. What could I do with a computer?"

"We could get you a typing program so you could learn to type," said Ryan. "Mary Elizabeth is a writer," he explained to Zack and Madison.

"A horse and a computer," she nodded. "I like it!" And so began her entry to the twenty-first-century world. A lot better than she had expected.

CHAPTER THIRTY-TWO

SINCE IT WAS Sunday, Zack said that he had some extra money—twenty-first-century as well as nineteenth-century—to tide Mary Elizabeth over until he had a chance to sell her two coins to the dealer. And while Madison explained all the kitchen appliances to her, Zack paid Ryan the money from the last coins that he had dropped off.

Then Madison's phone rang, so Zack explained all about cell phones to Mary Elizabeth while Ryan just smiled. He could be happy just gazing at her face forever. Through a dreamy haze, he heard Madison say, "No, I don't know anyone who would want one. Oh, wait!" She walked over to Ryan and gently pushed him out of hearing range of Mary Elizabeth. "She loves dogs, Ryan. Want to get her a puppy? They're great dogs, I know the parents. Golden Retrievers! What do you think?"

Ryan smiled at his niece and hugged her. "You're awesome! Yes, it's perfect! Can you pick one out so I can surprise her when we return?"

"Sure, Ryan." Madison walked into the other room to finish her conversation.

Meanwhile, Zack and Mary Elizabeth sat on the couch in front of a laptop, with Zack showing her how everything worked. When Ryan walked over, she looked up at him and said, "I like this place, Ryan. Thank you for bringing me."

"Are you about ready? We still have several places to go today." He held out his hand to help her up.

"Sure! Thanks, Zack, for showing me everything."

"Bye, Zack, tell Madison good-bye and thank you," said Ryan, as he escorted Mary Elizabeth out.

"Bye," she called over her shoulder as they walked out the door.

Ryan took her hand into both of his and looked at her. "Now, are you ready to ride in a car? I'm a good driver."

"I'm more ready now than I was!"

He opened the car door for her, helped her inside, and showed her how to put on the seat belt. Then he walked around to the other side and stepped in.

"What's this for, anyway?" She pulled the seat belt out to show him.

"It's a seat belt. It holds you in place in case there's an accident. But accidents aren't that common, so it's not something that you have to worry about."

"I'm worried, anyway."

Ryan started the car, and Mary Elizabeth jumped at the sound and looked nervous. He put his hand on her hand and smiled gently. "When you were a girl, was there ever an accident with horses where someone got hurt?"

"Yes, but I knew that Cookie wouldn't do that to me, so I wasn't afraid."

"Wasn't there ever a case where there were several horses together and one horse did something bad and it affected another horse and caused an accident?"

Mary Elizabeth nodded her head. "Yeah. One time a bunch of us were riding, and someone slipped off, and her horse took off and slammed into my friend Phyllis's horse. She was a sweet little mare, but she got knocked sideways, Phyllis fell off, and her mare stepped on her accidentally."

"So, you see that accidents happen, but not often. Cars go faster than horses, though, so we need seat belts to keep us safe. Are you ready to go?"

"Yes, I suppose so."

Ryan backed out of the driveway and into the street. He glanced over at Mary Elizabeth, who seemed more relaxed than a minute before.

"*This* isn't faster than a horse!" she said, smiling.

Ryan chuckled. "No, but if you're interested, we can drive up on the highway so you can see how fast a car can go!"

"I think I'm fine with this," she said, smiling back at him. "For now."

Ryan chuckled again. "You *are* the adventurous one!"

"I get skeery, but I get over it pretty quick."

"I see that!" Ryan nodded and smiled. "Okay, here we are. First stop."

Mary Elizabeth had been looking at both sides of the street as they drove. Now she turned her head where Ryan was looking and read aloud. "Second Time Around Thrift Store. What is it?"

"It's a place to buy clothes and all kinds of other items. I buy stuff here and then resell it at the shop—usually for a loss, but at least I'm helpful. Come on, let's go in."

He got out of the car, walked around, opened her

door, showed her how to unhook her seat belt, and helped her out. They walked into the thrift store, and she looked around.

"It's as big as stores in Atlanta!"

"Go ahead. Look around. Everything in here is used, but it's mostly in good condition. I'm just going to pick up a few things." Ryan didn't have anything on his list to pick up for people, but he always checked to see if there was anything that he thought would sell. He stopped in front of the men's rack to look around, while Mary Elizabeth walked around the store. Every few minutes he'd look up to check on her, and she would be wandering around with a big smile on her face. He loved making her happy.

CHAPTER THIRTY-THREE

Although Ryan had told her that everything in the store was used, it all looked good to her. It reminded her of the large stores in Atlanta, so she felt at home here. She had money in her pocket, and she could buy anything she wanted. She picked out a couple of long skirts and two blouses to go with them. Now that she worked at the hotel, she should have more clothes. Then she picked up two leather purses that she liked. After that, she wandered over to the other part of the store with dishes and pots and pans. Shrugging her shoulders, she picked up a plate that had a divider in the middle. Her mother would like that. Although she still believed that it was her mother who should apologize to her, Mary Elizabeth thought she could give it to her to smooth everything over.

"You ready to check out?" asked Ryan, holding some pants and shirts.

"Sure! I have a few things here."

After they had paid for their purchases and were back inside the car, Mary Elizabeth looked at Ryan and said, "Thank you, Ryan. I'm having such a great time here! How could you ever leave?"

"Easy," said Ryan. "If I hadn't left, I would have never met you." He smiled at her in a way that made her sigh. "How much money did Zack give you?"

She looked into her purse and pulled out a stack of hundred dollar bills. After counting them twice, she said, "Three thousand dollars. Why?"

"Were you serious about wanting a computer?"

"Yeah!"

"Well, let's go! Then when we get back to the house, Zack can download a typing program so you can learn to type."

"Awesome!"

Ryan laughed. "You're just getting too twenty-first-century for me, now!"

They parked in front of the Apple Store, and Ryan held the door open for her to walk in first. She could not believe what it looked like inside. There were computers of all shapes and sizes, the little music thing that Jenna had, and many more shiny and bright objects. When Ryan saw her looking at the music things, he said, "Let's get your computer first and then look at the iPods."

Ryan guided her up to the counter. "We'd like to see the newest Mac laptop, please."

The man at the counter placed a metallic computer in front of her. It had a picture of an apple on top of it. When Mary Elizabeth just stared at it, the man opened it and the screen lit up. When he started talking about the internal workings of the computer, Ryan said to him, "Listen, she's a newbie. She doesn't understand any of that. But we'd like one just like this with upgraded memory." Then he looked at her. "Right, Mary Elizabeth? You want it, right?"

She nodded her head up and down, up and down like

it had a mind of its own. "Yes, definitely!"

The man brought her a large box with a suitcase-type handle and laid it on the counter. "Anything else?"

"Do you see an iPod that you want?" Ryan asked, as he pointed to the display in the glass case beneath them.

"I want one just like Jenna's, except blue. That one there! And upgraded memory, please." She didn't know what it meant, but if it was good for the computer, it must be good for the iPod, too.

Ryan smiled at the man. "Double the regular hard drive."

"Thirty-two gigs?" asked the man.

"Sure, that's fine. Mary Elizabeth, I really think you should get one of these, too." Ryan moved to the counter on their left.

"It looks neat, but what is it?"

"It's called an iPad," said Ryan.

"What does it do?"

"A lot of things, but you can play games on it," said Ryan.

"Games?"

The man behind the counter turned around, picked one up from behind him, touched the front of it, and suddenly there was movement all over the screen. "Games like this," he said.

"That's some pumpkins!" said Mary Elizabeth, delighted.

"Do you think you want one?" asked Ryan.

She nodded. "Might as well go the whole hog!"

Ryan looked at the man behind the counter. "Can I see the specs on this model, please?" When the man handed him a sheet of paper, Ryan ran his hand down the writing and then said, "Sixty-four gigs, but can we get one without wifi or cell?"

"*Why* would you want one like *that*?" the man asked.

Ryan shrugged. "Where we come from, well, we can't use those, anyway."

"Oh, I want the regular one, Ryan. So I can use it when we're here."

"Okay, we'll take this one."

While the man turned around and tapped keys on a machine, Ryan turned to her. "Do you have the money?"

When the man gave her a slip of paper with the amount she owed on it, she counted it out in all one hundred dollar bills. Ryan smiled at her. "You're a computer owner, now!"

As the man counted the bills, he said, "All hundreds, huh? You guys drug dealers or something?"

Ryan laughed. "Nothing like that at all. We just hit a big payday, that's all." He turned to Mary Elizabeth. "You ready to go, my lady? I'll carry this big box; you can put this one in your purse," he said. Then he picked up the iPad and handed her the iPod.

"Where are we going now?" she asked, as they walked out of the store.

"The grocery store. Wait till you see it! I bet it's bigger even than the stores in Atlanta!" After loading everything from the Apple Store onto the floor of the back seat and helping Mary Elizabeth into the car, he stepped in himself, started the car, pulled out into traffic, and proceeded down the road. Several minutes later, he pulled into a large area where many cars were parked in front of a big building.

"Is this it? It's huge!"

Ryan smiled. "I told you!"

When they walked inside, Ryan took a cart and

pushed it over in front of her. "This place is really big. I think we should stay together so you don't get lost."

"I agree!" she said, putting her hands on the shopping cart and following him down the aisle. Looking around, she was amazed that such a huge place would contain only food. Shelf after shelf of all kinds of food. They stopped in front of a display of pickles, and there were not only many varieties, but the same variety in different bottles. When they arrived at the other side of the store, there was a huge area with only fruit and vegetables! She couldn't believe it. Even foods that she hadn't seen since Atlanta were displayed all over. Ryan had put two bags of oranges in the basket, and she smiled when she saw them. But when she discovered a display of pineapples, she couldn't contain her excitement. "I've had one of these before! I love them! Can I buy it?"

"You can buy anything you want, Mary Elizabeth. Anything."

She put it in the basket and followed him into a line where you paid for your purchases. There was a long row of them—places to pay—and people lined up in front of each one. Ryan put the food on something that would move so the cashier could reach all the items. This place was so magical! How could she ever go home again after this? Her mood darkened. The nineteenth century held nothing for her now—not after seeing all the bright lights, fancy objects, and just plain miracles all around her.

"I'll pay for your pineapple, Mary Elizabeth. No prob-lem."

Smiling at him, she tried to swallow and found that she couldn't. "Water," she croaked, "I need some water."

"It's right down there, Miss. Right past customer service."

"It's okay, Mary Elizabeth. I'll meet you there."

Squeezing past him, she stumbled into the broad aisle and stood in front of something that looked like water came out of it. When she pushed the button, water flowed out. Leaning down to drink, she didn't think she could ever return to the nineteenth century. She didn't want to. Ever again. To her mother who called her a spinster, and her father who treated her like a nonentity. No reason to go back. Ever.

Just then, Ryan pushed the cart up beside her. "Are you okay? You looked kind of pale back there."

"I'm fine now." Taking another big swallow of water, she walked out with him to the car.

Ryan opened the back door of the car and placed the food into a large container. "This keeps the food cold. I have one in the wagon, too, but it's disguised."

Back in the car again, Ryan said, "I wanted to take you out for lunch, er, dinner, but I'm not hungry at all yet, are you?"

She shook her head. "No."

"We'll go back to the house now and maybe we'll go out later."

Mary Elizabeth was silent all the way back to the house. She wondered what Ryan would think of her so quiet like that, but she had to think. The more she thought of it, the more she realized that she wanted to stay here in the twenty-first century. Although she had grown used to the slow, easy lifestyle of small town Red Bluff, the new Red Bluff was a city like she remembered the nineteenth-century Atlanta to be. And she liked that. Could she ever return to the nineteenth century and be happy again?

151

But there was something else to think about. Ryan. There was one thing that she knew for certain. She wanted to be wherever he was. Would he want to move back here—back to where he had come from? Although she didn't know the answer to that question, she hoped for the best. As they pulled up in front of the ranch house, she looked at him, patted his hand, and smiled.

CHAPTER THIRTY-FOUR

RYAN PARKED THE car, helped Mary Elizabeth out, and grabbed the packages in the back. Mary Elizabeth was still strangely silent and didn't even offer to help him carry the packages—not that he needed the help, but he expected her to be excited enough to want to carry the computer herself. Well, maybe it was just a nineteenth-century thing. He wasn't going to worry about it.

As they approached the house, Ryan wondered if Madison had a chance to pick up the puppy. He noticed that Madison's car and Zack's little truck were both in the driveway, so he knocked on the door to let her know to hide the puppy before they entered. Zack answered the door.

"Hi! Come on in. Madison is in the bedroom, um, on the phone." He winked at Ryan. "Wow! What all did you buy? Looks like you hit the jackpot!"

When Mary Elizabeth didn't answer, Ryan said, "She got the latest laptop, a new iPod, and an iPad. I think she's all set! Zack would you start up the computer for the first time, get it going, and then install a good typing program?"

153

"Is that all right, Mary Elizabeth? You don't mind me starting up your computer first?" Zack looked at her.

She nodded dreamily and looked around the room at the television and stereo. When Zack gave Ryan a questioning look, Ryan just shrugged. He didn't know why she was acting like that. Was she feeling okay? He hoped so. Ryan looked at Zack when Mary Elizabeth was looking the other way, and mouthed the words, "Did you get the puppy?" When Zack nodded, Ryan said, "Mary Elizabeth, why don't you sit down? I have a surprise for you."

"All right." She sat on the couch and continued staring at the television.

Ryan walked to the back bedroom and found Madison on the phone, the puppy fast asleep beside her. When she saw him, she immediately got off the phone. "Oh, she's gorgeous!" said Ryan.

"She's a he, but yes he is!"

"I want to bring him right out to Mary Elizabeth right now! She's feeling a little weird since we went to the grocery store, and I'm hoping he will cheer her up."

"Let me go out, first, and talk to her a minute, okay?"

Madison walked out of the room, down the hallway, and into the living room. Ryan could hear her talking to Mary Elizabeth, but he couldn't make out the words. He wondered how long he should wait. Then he heard them coming turning the corner into the hallway, so he quickly angled the door so she couldn't look in. Madison showed her the bathroom, showed her how to flush the toilet, and use the sink. After Mary Elizabeth closed the bathroom door, Madison walked back into the bedroom.

"When she comes out and gets settled back in the living room, why don't you bring out the puppy? And she

154

seemed fine when I showed her the bathroom."

"Maybe it's just been a long day for her. She didn't say anything on the drive home and stayed quiet when we came inside the house."

When they heard the toilet flush, Madison said, "I'm going back in there now. See you in a minute! I'm sure she's going to love him!" She glanced at the puppy, still peacefully sleeping on the bed. "Oh! You know what? When he wakes up, he's going to want to piddle. Why don't you take him out the back door before bringing him out?"

"Sure. I'll do it now." He picked up the puppy in his arms, and it squirmed about and licked him on the face. Opening the back door of the room as quietly as he could, he slipped outside and put the puppy on the grass. After he finished, Ryan kneeled down, praised the puppy lavishly, and picked him up again. Holding him still while he walked through the door was a chore, but he managed to get inside, close the door quietly, and walk to the half-closed bedroom door. Peering down the hallway to see if the bathroom door was open again, he saw that it was, so he walked to the edge of the hallway, still hidden behind the wall.

"Mary Elizabeth? Are you ready for your surprise?"

"I guess so," she said.

"Okay, here he comes!" Ryan walked into the living room and set the puppy on the ground.

Mary Elizabeth, sitting on the edge of the couch, leaned over, and the puppy ran right for her. "Oh, he's gorgeous! What a little cutie!" She looked at Madison, who sat next to her. "Is he yours, Madison?" When Madison shook her head, Mary Elizabeth looked at Ryan.

"He's *yours*, Mary Elizabeth! That's your surprise. I got you a puppy! He's all yours!"

"Oh, Ryan! I love him! Thank you!" She gathered the puppy up in her arms, hugging him, and then stood up and hugged Ryan, the puppy in between them licking both their faces in turn.

Mary Elizabeth kneeled on the floor playing with the puppy, and alternately hugging him and being licked in the face by him. "He's perfect. What should I name him?"

"He's your puppy, Mary Elizabeth. You choose," said Ryan.

"He looks like a little bear, so I'm going to name him Bear! Come here, Bear!" the puppy jumped up onto her and licked her in the face again. "He already knows his name!"

Madison, Zack, and Ryan all laughed. Then Ryan first and Madison and Zack all joined her on the floor to play with the puppy. After an hour of playing, the puppy finally fell to the floor exhausted. Everyone laughed and returned to the couch.

Ryan checked his watch. "Oh, it's getting late. We better get you home, Mary Elizabeth. Sorry we don't have time for me to take you out for dinner."

Mary Elizabeth, looking at the sleeping puppy on the floor, said, "It's okay. I would have rather had him, anyway."

"Do you want me to make you some sandwiches for the way home?" asked Madison.

"That would be great! Thank you!" answered Ryan. "Mary Elizabeth, I think we should leave all your electronics here so Zack can get them ready for you. Is that okay?"

"Can I take the music one home? I'd really like to listen to some music," she said, without taking her eyes off the sleeping puppy.

"It doesn't have any music on it, yet. That's something Zack will do for you. Then next time we come back, everything will be all set for you. Although if your father finds the computer in your room, I don't know what he'd say about it." Ryan stood up.

"Oh, yeah. You're right. And, oh, no. He won't let me have the puppy, either!" She looked up at Ryan, worried.

"I'll keep him at my place, but he'll be all yours!" In his mind, Ryan was thinking *ours* after I ask you to marry me.

"Thank you, Ryan." She stood up and hugged Ryan again. "You're so good to me."

"Sandwiches are ready!" Madison walked into the living room and handed Mary Elizabeth four sandwiches in plastic sandwich bags.

Mary Elizabeth looked at the sandwich bags in her hands. "Whatever are these?"

"Sandwiches!" said Madison.

"No, what the sandwiches are in."

"Oh! More twentieth-century stuff, Mary Elizabeth! It's called plastic, and it's *everywhere!*"

"Oh. Okay." Just another amazing thing that she liked about being in the future. "Ryan? Would you hold the sandwiches so I can carry the puppy?" She handed the sandwiches to Ryan.

"Sure! See you guys later!" Ryan headed for the door.

"It was good seeing you again, Zack. And nice meeting you, Madison! Thanks for everything!" Mary Elizabeth picked up the puppy and followed Ryan toward the door.

157

Zack called out, "Bye! See you later! I'll cash in the coins and get all your stuff ready for you! Bye!"

Madison walked up behind them. "Nice meeting you, too, Mary Elizabeth. And you're welcome here anytime! With or without Ryan." She smiled warmly at Mary Elizabeth, who turned around and hugged her, puppy and all.

"Oh! I still have to load the stuff! I forgot all about it! I'll be right back!" Then Ryan hesitated, turned around, and called into the house, "Hey, Zack, would you give me a hand with this stuff?"

Ryan walked out to the car and gathered up everything he bought at the thrift store and Mary Elizabeth's purchases. When Zack appeared, Ryan said, "Can you get the cooler?" They carried everything out to the wagon, and Ryan exchanged the cooler that Zack carried for the one in the wagon. "Can you put that one back in my car for me, please?"

"Sure, man. See ya later," said Zack, as he walked away.

"Send Mary Elizabeth out, will ya?" Ryan called Dolly in from the pasture—she was good about that—and harnessed her up to the wagon. When Mary Elizabeth arrived, puppy in arms and a huge smile on her face, he took the puppy from her, helped her up into the wagon, and handed the puppy back to her.

Ryan climbed into the wagon, and they took off. He opened the gates while Mary Elizabeth guided Dolly through with one hand, the other hand struggling to hold the puppy, which made her laugh. She kept cuddling the puppy and talking to him, in between thanking Ryan for giving him to her. He thought he would have a chance to ask her on the way home, but they were at the cave in no time, and the only conversation they had was puppy-related. Oh, well, he thought, when they finally pulled up in front of his store, he'd have time later.

CHAPTER THIRTY-FIVE

Ryan had given her the new clothes that she bought, gently wrapped around her mother's new dish and placed in the large saddlebags that he loaned her. The pineapple and oranges were in the other compartment. He was going to give her something called a backpack, but said that her father probably wouldn't approve—although Ryan wondered what he would say about the oranges and the pineapple. Mary Elizabeth was hoping that he would just say thank you.

As she climbed into the wagon after Ezra had harnessed Old Cookie for her, she looked down the street at where Ryan's store was. He was still out there, holding Bear, and waving to her and then holding up Bear's little paw so it looked like he was waving, too. Mary Elizabeth smiled and waved, and then Old Cookie started for home. She was so excited about Bear on the way home, that she forgot that she had wanted to tell Ryan about how she felt about the new Red Bluff—how she wanted to move there, and hoped that he would want to return there as well.

Now as she turned for home, she thought about her

conversation with Madison while Ryan was harnessing up Dolly. Madison had said that Dolly actually belonged to Jenna, technically, but Granny was the one who occasionally rode her, and then Ryan took her on the weekend to buy supplies. Madison also told her that if she asked, Granny would probably let her ride her, and then Mary Elizabeth could come visit even without Ryan, because Dolly knew exactly which way to go. The idea excited Mary Elizabeth—going to the future all by herself! Was she brave enough? She wasn't sure; she wasn't sure at all.

After pulling into the driveway, Mary Elizabeth put the wagon where it was kept, unhooked Old Cookie from the harness, and walked her into the barn to brush her. When she finished, she walked to the wagon, grabbed the saddlebags, and entered the house. She smiled as she thought about giving her mother the new bowl and giving her father the pineapple. Reaching into the saddlebags, she pulled the pineapple out and then heard her father's footsteps behind her. Turning with a smile, she held out the pineapple to him.

Anger erupted out of him when he saw her face. Knocking the pineapple out of her hands and onto the floor, he shouted, "You *lied* to me! You didn't work today! I stopped in to see you at the hotel, and that old woman said you weren't there." His eyes narrowed at her, and his mouth tightened. "You *lied* to me," he repeated.

She glanced at the pineapple on the floor, toppled over, and then looked at him. "I didn't lie to you," she said calmly. "I worked *yesterday*, and I never said that I was going to work today. You didn't ask."

"*Where* were you? And where did you get that?" He pointed to the pineapple.

161

"I was with Ryan. You know, the mudsill who has gone to *college* and gotten a *degree*."

"I have already told you that I did not want you associating with him—degree or not," he said through clenched teeth. "And where did he get that? Did he steal it?"

At first she was so shocked at his sudden outburst that she was shaken. But now, she had hold of herself. "I'm not even going to honor that with a response." Reaching into the saddlebags, she pulled out the bag of oranges and set them on the floor. Reaching into the other side, she unwrapped the new dish she had gotten her mother and gently put that on the floor beside the oranges. "That"—she pointed to the bowl—"is for Mama." Then she walked into her bedroom and slammed the door.

Her father pounded on the door with his fist. "I will have answers out of you! You *will* give me answers! And don't even think about using the wagon again to go to your *job*. You can walk! If you really *have* a job." He hit the door one more time with his fist and then walked away.

Mary Elizabeth flung herself on her bed intending to cry, but the tears wouldn't come. She was way too angry for that. How dare he treat her like that! How dare he speak to her that way! Immediately, she knew the course of action she had to take—she had known it all day. This outrage just confirmed it. She was moving to the new Red Bluff and leaving his anger and bitterness behind.

CHAPTER THIRTY-SIX

ALTHOUGH IT WAS still morning, Ryan had expected Mary Elizabeth to come see Bear before she started work. And she *must* have started by now. He looked at the puppy asleep at his feet. Of course you're asleep, you little devil, he thought. You kept me up all night whining and crying! Ryan frowned. Where was Mary Elizabeth?

The front door opened. Ryan peered out from the easel to see Nick walk in.

"Hey, Ryan!"

"Hey, Nick. How's it going?"

"Lovin' it here in the nineteenth century, man!"

Bear woke up and bounded from the back room and jumped up on Nick. "Who's this little cutie?" He knelt down to pet the puppy.

"That's Bear. I gave him to Mary Elizabeth yesterday."

"Where'd you get him? I didn't hear of any dog in town having puppies."

"Not in *this* town, maybe. We went to the *other* town yesterday."

163

"You told her already? I didn't know you were going to tell her so soon."

"Turns out, it wasn't my decision at all. Mary Elizabeth and I went to dinner at Josiah and Jenna's, and *they* decided it would be a good idea. They didn't give me much of a choice."

"But if you went to *town* yesterday with her, then she must have taken it well."

"Yeah. She wanted to go right away. And while we were there, she bought a laptop, an iPod, and an iPad! Zack's fixing them for her."

"Where'd she get the money for that? I know her father's loaded, but that's nineteenth-century money."

When Nick stood up, the puppy wandered back to Ryan and was just about to piddle, when Ryan swept him up. "I'll be right back." A minute later, Ryan came back in and set the puppy down. "It's starting to snow out there. Anyone come in?"

"No," said Nick.

"Mary Elizabeth found a coin at the bank worth nearly twenty thousand dollars! She wants to buy a horse, now."

"I'm going to have to get one of Zack's lists. But honestly, as long as I'm living here—and I'm not planning to leave—I don't really need much money. What I need is a woman! I think you got the last single woman in town! I was hoping that I wouldn't have to go back to the new Red Bluff to find a woman, but I may have to. I'm tired of eating my own cooking."

Just then, the front door opened and Rachel walked in. "Hey, Ryan. Hey, Nick. Ryan, you have a ream of paper by any chance? Hey, who's this?" she asked when the puppy ran up to her.

"That's Bear, Mary Elizabeth's puppy. I have a partial ream upstairs with my printer. But I can give it to you, if you want."

"That'd be awesome, Ryan! Thanks!"

Ryan ran upstairs and came down a minute later with an almost full ream of paper. "Will this work for you?"

"Sure, perfect," she said without standing up. "This puppy is adorable! Where'd you get him?"

"One of Madison's friends."

"Oh! Over *there*!" She stood up. "Well, I better get back. See ya!" Then she ran out again.

"Do I know her? She knows me. *Should* I know her?" he said with a guilty expression on his face.

Ryan laughed. "I don't think you've ever been out with her, if that's what you mean. She's a friend of Jenna's. She's probably seen you around. That's all. Hey, there's a woman for you!"

"You mean one of Jenna's friends from *there* or here?"

"*There*. Why? What does it matter?"

"I prefer a nineteenth-century woman."

"Nick, you're way too picky."

The front door flew open and an angry Mr. Mills strolled through the door. "Where is she?" he demanded.

"Who?" asked Ryan, confused.

"I'll be leaving now," said Nick, scurrying out the door.

"You know dratted well who I'm talking about! Mary Elizabeth!"

"She's working today as far as I know."

The puppy ran up to Mr. Mills and jumped on him. "What's this? Get this mutt away from me!"

He pulled back his leg as if to kick the puppy, and

Ryan shouted at him. "If you kick that dog, Sir, I swear I'll hit you in the mouth." He said it respectfully, but his face was grim, and he held out a fist in front of him.

"Just get him away from me! And tell me where she is!"

Ryan called Bear and picked him up. "If she's not working, then I have no idea where she is, Mr. Mills. Did you ask Granny?"

"She said that she borrowed her horse and said she wouldn't be working today. If she's not with you, where would she be? Especially in this weather."

Ryan looked out the window and saw that the snow had gotten heavier. "I don't know where she is. Maybe she rode out to see my sister, Jenna."

"Where's that?" Mr. Mills asked. His demeanor had softened.

"Out just west of town. But let me go next door and ask Josiah." Ryan carried the puppy past Mr. Mills and walked out the door. Mr. Mills followed. Opening the door to Josiah's office, Ryan and Mr. Mills walked in.

Josiah sat at his desk, with Nick sitting in a chair beside him reading a magazine. They both looked up when the door opened.

"Hey, Ryan. Mr. Mills. How can I help you? Cute puppy!" Josiah's dog, Bingo, walked over to smell the puppy, and Bear struggled to get free from Ryan's arms.

"Josiah, when did you get into town?" Ryan asked.

"Funny question," said Josiah. "About five minutes ago, why?"

"Did Mary Elizabeth go to see Jenna? Or did you maybe see her on the road?"

"Nope. Didn't see her. Why? She missing?"

Ryan glanced at Mr. Mills, who had a frantic expres-

166

sion on his face. "I guess she is, yeah. She was supposed to work today, but wasn't there."

Josiah stole a quick glance at Ryan, but looked at Mr. Mills. "Would you like me to investigate, sir?"

"No, thank you," said Ryan. "I'll handle it. I have an idea, so I'll go look for her. Nick would you mind watching the store—and the puppy? In a couple hours, feed him half a cup of the food I have upstairs, okay?"

Nick stood up and took the puppy out of Ryan's arms. "Sure thing, Ryan. No problem." Then he glanced at Josiah. "If you need me, I'll be next door." Josiah nodded.

Ryan glanced out the window. The snow was heavier still. "I'm going to get my jacket, then I'll get my horse and go." He opened the door and hurried next door covering his face with his hands.

"I'm coming with you!" Mr. Mills was right behind him.

Ryan turned quickly as they entered the store. "No! I'll go by myself."

"She's my only daughter!" he pleaded. "And I'm afraid she ran away because of me."

"Why would you say that?"

"We had an argument last night. I was angry and took it out on her."

Ryan's hands involuntarily balled up into fists again. "You didn't hit her, did you?"

Mr. Mills looked at the floor and shook his head. "No. I'm worried about her."

Ryan put his hand on the man's shoulder. "So am *I*. And I'll take care of it. I'll let you know as soon as I know something."

"Take my horse, Ryan. He's fast."

167

Ryan shook his head. "Thank you, but fast isn't going to matter in weather like this."

CHAPTER THIRTY-SEVEN

HE RAN UPSTAIRS to get his heavy winter parka and slipped it on as he stepped out the back door. Running all the way to the livery with an arm in front of his eyes, he couldn't tell for sure, but Ryan thought—and hoped —that the snow had slowed down. When he got to the livery, he shouted, "Ezra, I'm in a hurry! Can you get my saddle for me, please?"

By the time Ryan had finished brushing his horse, a big sorrel gelding named Treetop, Ezra had brought not only the saddle and blanket, but the bridle as well. "Why're you going out on a day like this?" asked Ezra, looking at the snow building up outside.

"Mary Elizabeth is missing."

"She's on Dolly. She left this morning before it started to snow. I hope she's okay."

"Thanks, Ezra! Bye!"

Ryan nudged the reluctant horse forward into the storm. Patting him on the side of the neck, he said, "We're going to your old home, boy. I sure hope you can find it."

The snow had abated, which Ryan was grateful for.

But when he reached the side trail to the cave, too much snow had fallen for him to see if there were tracks. They walked into the cave, and it was a brief respite from the storm. Very brief.

Emerging on the other side of the cave, he encountered the heaviest snow yet. Ryan could barely see in front of him, and he had no idea how Treetop would ever find his way home. "Hope you can use that horsey-instinct to find the way, Treetop, because I won't be any help at all. I'm already lost, and we're only steps away from the cave." The horse plowed on through the storm with his head down, and when he veered left, Ryan hoped they were on the main trail. "You're doing good, big fella. Really good. Almost there now."

It took Ryan and Treetop longer to reach the gate than he remembered, but they were also going slower. Accompanying the heavy snow was a strong wind that blew snow in their faces. Going through the gates, Ryan rode up to the barn, hopped off, and led Treetop inside. He put him in one of the stalls, taking off his bridle, and then brushing all the still wet snow off him. "Rest while you can, boy, I don't think we'll be here for long."

The stall next to Treetop contained Dolly who nickered when she saw him. "Hello, girl," he said and petted her on the nose. "So glad to see you!" The sight of her relaxed him, because although this is where he thought that Mary Elizabeth had gone, he wasn't confident about it until he saw Dolly. He slowly shook his head and closed his eyes. "She's safe. She's safe."

He walked out of the barn, across the driveway and up to the front door, which he opened without knocking. Taking off the heavy parka and giving it a couple shakes to get the snow off, he left it on a hook by the door.

When he walked into the living room, he saw Mary Elizabeth and Zack completely concentrating on a video game.

Zack looked up. "I thought I heard the front door open. What're you doing out in this weather?"

Mary Elizabeth picked up her head and looked at who Zack was talking to. Seeing Ryan, she jumped up and hugged him. "Ryan! What are you doing here?"

"Looking for you, Mary Elizabeth. What are *you* doing here?"

"My father treated me horribly last night when I got home." She looked at Ryan with a sad face. "He threw the pineapple that I got him down on the floor, and said bad things about you, and accused me of lying to him about having a job." Then she looked down with her hands folded in front of her. "I can't take it anymore, Ryan. I had to leave, and I want to move here, anyway."

"Oh, Mary Elizabeth. Your father was frantic with worry. He's very remorseful now and wanted to come with me to find you. He even offered to let me ride his horse!"

"*Rojo*? He offered to let you ride Rojo? That *is* something."

"Yeah, and now that I know you're safe, I need to go back and tell him."

"Oh, no, Ryan. It's not safe out there. You need to stay here until the snow stops," said Mary Elizabeth.

Madison walked out from the back bedroom. "Did I hear you say you're going back today? Ryan, you're soaking wet. You could die out there! Come on, take off your pants and let me put them in the dryer."

Ryan looked down at his pant legs. The snow had melted and was now dripping down onto the floor. He was soaked and cold. "Okay, give me a robe. But as soon as they're dry, I have to leave. When is the snow supposed to stop?"

"Not until about nine tonight—if you can trust the weather service. This was supposed to only be a dusting!"

Five minutes later, Ryan was wearing one of Zack's robes, and his pants were in the dryer. Sitting down next to Mary Elizabeth, he said, "Did Zack get your computer and stuff all fixed up the way you want?"

"Yes, it's awesome!" Mary Elizabeth beamed. "And he gave me this!" She picked up an iPhone from the coffee table and handed it to him.

"An iPhone? Zack? You gave her your iPhone?"

"No, it's my iPhone," said Madison. "My old one. When I broke the screen, I got another one. Zack fixed this one, and we were going to sell it on eBay, but Mary Elizabeth can have it."

"Why does she need it?" Ryan looked confused.

Mary Elizabeth couldn't look at him. "I told you, Ryan. I want to move here. Do you think you would consider moving back here?" She looked at him hopefully.

"Oh, Mary Elizabeth. You're just upset. Wait until you settle down before you make a decision like that. And did Zack tell you how hard it was for him to move here?" He looked at Zack. "You need to tell her exactly how it happened, Zack, and why it can't happen again. But not now. I need some diversion while I'm waiting." He picked up the video control that Mary Elizabeth had put down. "I'm going to kick your butt, Zack. What are you and Madison doing home, anyway? Don't you have school today?"

"Classes were canceled because of the snow." Zack set up the game and said, "Here we go!"

An hour and many video games later, Ryan had his pants back on and was looking out the window. "I don't know how that horse is going to find its way home, but it has to."

"Hey, Ryan, if you insist on riding back in this weather, take my GPS. I'm not sure how much it will help you, though. You can follow the trail back to the cave. It won't work on the other side of the cave, but it should get you there."

Mary Elizabeth stood up and gripped his hand. "Ryan. It's not safe for you to go. I'll worry about you."

He looked at her and kissed her on the nose. "Like I worried about you. You didn't even say good-bye to me *or* Bear."

"Bear! How is Bear? *Where* is Bear?"

"Nick's taking care of him. Zack show me what to do again with this thing." When the brief lesson was completed, Ryan put on his parka and put the GPS in the pocket. "I hope it's waterproof."

"It is," said Zack.

"Ryan, how will I know you got there safely?" asked Mary Elizabeth. Then she turned and picked something up from the coffee table. "Take this! Call when you get home!"

Ryan, Zack, and Madison all laughed, but Mary Elizabeth didn't get the joke. "It doesn't work in the nineteenth century, Mary Elizabeth," said Madison. "But you can call when you reach the cave, Ryan. If that doesn't work, a text probably will. And both of our numbers are already in there."

He slipped it into the other pocket of his parka,

thanked them for their help and for taking care of Mary Elizabeth, and then he kissed Mary Elizabeth gently on the lips. "So I'll tell your father that he'll see you tomorrow morning?"

"No. I can't stand the thought of that. Tell him I'll be home late and see him at home."

"He'll probably be upset at that, but okay. See y'all later." He waved over his shoulder and walked out of the house. Five minutes later, he and Treetop were past the gates and on the main trail back toward the cave. "Now we're going to our *other* home, Treetop. Try your best, and I'll keep an eye on the trail with the GPS. Personally, I would trust horse sense better, but there is the chance that you'll want to detour and take me back to the barn you grew up in."

Part horse sense with a little GPS thrown in, they reached the cave without incident. Ryan was grateful that Treetop was so tall: seventeen hands or sixty-eight inches. He wasn't called Treetop for nothing. But some of those snowdrifts needed his long legs to get through them. At the entrance to the cave, Ryan took out the iPhone and tried to call, but couldn't get a signal. Then he tried texting, "at cave safe." There was no way to know if they got it or not unless he waited for a response. It had said, "message sent," but he had learned from experience that wasn't always true. But less than a minute later, Madison had texted back, "got it!" Relieved that Mary Elizabeth wouldn't have to worry, he and Treetop entered the cave, and when he came out the other side, the snow had stopped.

A few minutes later, he was at the livery talking with Ezra. "Will you dry him off and give him a good rubdown, maybe a hot mash? He was a really good boy today. Couldn't have asked for any better. Thanks, Ezra." Giving the horse a loving stroke on the head, he said, "And thank you, Treetop. You were awesome!" The horse nickered, and Ryan ran down the sopping street toward the store.

When he stepped in the back door shivering with cold from his soaked pants, he looked up to see Mr. Mills standing in his back room.

"I thought you were going to let me know as soon as you got back," he said indignantly.

"I had to take care of my horse first. And by the way, your daughter is fine, safe, and dry."

"Why didn't she come back with you?"

Ryan pointed toward his dripping clothes. "Would you really want her to come back in weather like this?"

"It stopped snowing an hour ago."

Ryan shrugged and looked away. He wasn't going to get into *that*. "It's still snowing where she is, that's why I'm soaked. She should be back tomorrow, though she said not till later and that she'd see you at home."

"Thank you for going to check on her. And you came back through the foul weather just to tell me she was okay?" Ryan nodded. Mr. Mills continued. "Few men would have done that. You're an honorable man. Now I see what Mary Elizabeth sees in you." He nodded his head and then motioned toward the painting in front of him. "Did you do this?" Mr. Mills stood in front of the not-yet finished portrait of Mary Elizabeth.

"Yes, I did."

"Can I buy it?"

"No. That one is for me. It's not for sale. I can do another one for you, if you like." He had never sold a painting before, but now was as good a time to start as

175

any.

"Yes, I would like that. One of me."

Ryan, wanting to get out of his wet clothes and trying to hold back his laughter at the man's response, said, "Fine. We'll talk about it later. I need to change clothes right now." He started up the stairs, and Mr. Mills called after him.

"Ryan, why don't you come to supper tomorrow night after Mary Elizabeth gets home? I appreciate what you did today. You didn't have to come back to tell me, but you did. Thank you for that. Would you consider coming to supper?"

"Yes, Mr. Mills, I will. Thank you. See you then." Ryan hurried to change his clothes so he could go next door to thank Nick and get the puppy back.

CHAPTER THIRTY-EIGHT

MARY ELIZABETH GAZED out the window at the heavily falling snow wondering if Ryan would even make it through the storm, until Madison got the text that he was at the cave. Then she reluctantly walked over and sat next to Zack. "Please tell me the story of when you moved here. I want to hear everything."

For the next hour, Zack, assisted by Madison, told the whole story starting from when Zack got shot and ending when Kat called her friend at the U.S. Marshal's office—a one-time event that could not possibly happen again. Madison shrugged and looked at Mary Elizabeth with sympathy. "So you see, there is no way you could live her legally."

Mary Elizabeth hung her head until the words sank in. "What about illegally? Could I live here illegally? What if I was with Ryan?"

Zack shook his head. "No. Madison and I checked into that, too. Even if Ryan married you, you would still need to provide identification from where you were *from*. And since where you're *from* doesn't officially exist, it just wouldn't work, Mary Elizabeth. Sorry." He patted Madison's leg and hugged her to him. "I got really lucky, and I know it."

"But I could live here illegally as long as I didn't get caught, right?"

"Oh, Mary Elizabeth. You're just asking for it then. If you got caught, it would be a mess. Who knows where they might deport you to—Mexico, Iran? It could be a lot worse than living at your folks' house."

Mary Elizabeth leaned over and put her hands over her face. "I'm going to my room now." When she had arrived at the ranch house several hours earlier, realizing that she wouldn't be going home because of the weather, Madison had showed her to the spare bedroom. Now she closed the door, propped the pillow up behind her, and sat on the bed with her new laptop practicing the typing program that Zack had downloaded for her. Even if she couldn't be a twenty-first-century woman, she could at least act like one. Now she had a computer, an iPod, and an iPad, and Madison and Zack had showed her how to use them all. Zack had showed her how to use google and the internet. She felt practically like she was born here.

When Madison knocked on her door to tell her that dinner was ready—they called supper dinner in the twenty-first century—she reluctantly came out to join them. They chitchatted about various topics, but none of them brought up her moving to the twenty-first century. Dinner tasted good—Zack was a good cook—and she helped Madison clean up, although with the newfangled dishwasher, there wasn't much to do.

After dinner, they watched a movie, and then Mary Elizabeth retired into her room. She wouldn't fit in Madison's pajamas, so they had loaned her a pair of

Zack's. When she had arrived that morning, she hadn't planned to stay overnight. She wasn't sure what she intended because she felt so upset, she just felt a terrible need to get out of the old Red Bluff. But now she was here, and she still had to go back and face that whole ugly scene again.

Although, she had to admit, just the notion that her father was remorseful felt monumental to her. Had he ever been remorseful before about how he had treated her? She couldn't remember one time. And had he not checked on her at the hotel, he probably wouldn't be now. So why did he check on her, she wondered. It didn't matter. He did, and he was remorseful, and that was that. He had even been decent to Ryan, and there was a lot to be said about that.

And something else had happened that evening after her father had left her nearly crying on the bed. A couple of hours later, she had heard footsteps in the hall—her mother's footsteps. Then a slip of paper was slid underneath her door. She didn't pick it up until the footsteps disappeared again, but when she did, the note surprised her. It said, *Dearest Mary Elizabeth. Thank you very much for the nice bowl. I appreciate you thinking of me. And I want you to know that in spite of everything, I still love you. Mama.* It wasn't exactly an apology, but it was probably as close as she was going to get to one.

After learning the entire home row on Zack's typing program and then playing games on her iPad for an hour, she was ready to sleep. She wasn't ready to give up her idea of moving to the twenty-first century, yet, but she had resigned herself to returning to the old Red Bluff and dealing with her problems.

Later, when she was toasty warm underneath the

electric blanket that Madison had explained to her, she wondered what it would be like to live in this time—this time of miracles, big stores, and interesting happenings. And she wondered again how Ryan would feel about moving back here. Then she fell asleep and dreamed of computers, machines that washed dishes and clothes, and Ryan holding her close to him.

When she awakened the following morning, she was disoriented. Nothing in the room seemed familiar to her until she felt the heat from the blanket, and then it all came back to her. Time to get back to the nineteenth century and whatever that held for her. She dreaded it— confronting her father, thanking her mother for the note —and then she thought of Bear, and Ryan, and a part of her wanted to go back.

After breakfast, Madison helped her to saddle Dolly, although she said she could. But she was grateful, because it had been many years, and she wasn't sure if she did remember how. Madison had said to give Dolly her head and she would lead her home—even through the deep snow. Dolly, too, had grown up in the barn at the ranch house, but she had gone back and forth many times since she had moved to the old Red Bluff. After they saddled Dolly, they left her in the stall, and both women returned to the house. "Zack and I need to get ready for school, but you're welcome to stay as long as you want. And Mary Elizabeth, even though you can't live here, you can come stay with us anytime. Really. I mean it. I feel like you're a sister to me. And don't forget to tighten Dolly's cinch before you go!" Then Madison hugged Mary Elizabeth making her feel like she had a family who really cared about her, instead of a family who treated her unkindly.

After Zack and Madison left, Mary Elizabeth sat on the couch with her laptop practicing her typing. She was picking it up quickly, and she liked the feel of her fingers on the keys. By the time the afternoon was half gone, she had eaten the sandwiches that Madison left for her, and she knew all the keys. Q and Z were still difficult for her, but she intended on practicing that section of the lessons over a few times to get better until she was quicker. But now, she had to say good-bye to the twenty-first century and return to the nineteenth. She wasn't looking forward to the probable confrontation with her father, and maybe even her mother, but she was looking forward to seeing Ryan and Bear. Leaving all her electronics behind— that's what Zack called them—she took a deep breath and resigned herself to going back home.

Mary Elizabeth tightened the cinch on Dolly, slipped on the bridle, climbed into the saddle, and they were off. Once they left the final gate behind, nothing looked familiar. Everything was covered with such deep and heavy snow that it was a white wilderness that all looked the same. Ryan's tracks had long since disappeared, because it had snowed for hours yesterday after he had left. She didn't know if they were lost or not, and she didn't know if she should even feel worried. She had to trust Dolly to know the way to the cave, but until they reached it, she wasn't sure. Then they were through it, and past the little side trail, and the Red Bluff sign was in front of her.

Since she didn't want her father to see her out of his window, she cut off the main road close to the corner and came out around back of Ryan's store. Mary Elizabeth dreaded going home and facing her parents after everything that had happened—in the old Red Bluff *and* the new Red Bluff. After tying Dolly to the back hitching post by Ryan's store, she walked in through the back door hoping that Ryan was alone. Bear ran out to greet her, crying and wiggling.

"Bear! You remember me!" She picked him up and hugged him to her.

"Of course he remembers you. You're his mother, aren't you?" Ryan stood there looking at her.

Putting Bear down, she stood up and hugged Ryan. "Thank you for everything, Ryan."

"For what?" He shrugged.

"I don't want to go home, Ryan. What am I going to do?"

"I've been thinking about that, Mary Elizabeth. I was thinking that you should stay at the hotel until—"

"Ryan! You in here? I'm ready to leave now. You want to give me the puppy, now?" Josiah ambled in to the back room, followed by Bingo. Bear ran up to Bingo, jumping on him and licking him all over.

"Why are you giving him the puppy?" asked Mary Elizabeth with fear in her eyes.

"Don't worry, Mary Elizabeth, it's not for keeps! He'll be back tomorrow. I just didn't want to leave him alone tonight." Ryan patted her on the shoulder, then stooped down, picked Bear up, and handed him to Josiah. "Thanks, Josiah. I'll see ya tomorrow. I appreciate it!"

"No problem. See you tomorrow. Bye, Mary Elizabeth." Josiah walked out leaving them alone.

"Where are you going tonight?" she asked him.

"I've been invited out to supper."

"Oh." She started walking toward the door. "I'll see you later then. Bye."

"Bye, Mary Elizabeth. See you soon."

She started untying Dolly when Ryan ran out the back. "Hey, I was thinking. I'll give you a ride after you drop Dolly off. Is that okay? Would you mind?"

Mary Elizabeth nodded. She didn't know who would invite him to supper, but it was just another blow when she was down. The only good thing is what he mentioned about her staying at the hotel. That was a great idea, and tomorrow when they talked more, she would ask him about it. Not tonight. She didn't want to talk about it with him on the brief ride home; she felt way too down for that. Not only had she lost her will to live in the old Red Bluff, but there was a chance that she had lost Ryan, too.

CHAPTER THIRTY-NINE

"GET UP ON Dolly, so you don't ruin your dress on the muddy streets." Ryan helped her up and handed her the reins. Noticing that she seemed quiet, he said, "Are you okay, Mary Elizabeth?"

"I'll be fine, Ryan. I just really don't want to be here—don't want to see my parents."

"I think this affected your father more than you realize. At the very least, he probably won't treat you like that again, because he'll be afraid that you'll leave again. He really was worried."

"Mary Elizabeth, Ryan," said Ezra when he saw them. "I'll look after Dolly. You want me to give her a hot mash, also, Ryan?"

"No, not yet, she still has some work to do. But if you could unsaddle her, I would appreciate it. I need her to pull the wagon."

"Ryan, how about if I loan you another horse who can pull the wagon? That way I can give Dolly a rub down and the hot mash."

"Ezra, have I told you lately how awesome you are?"

Ezra looked down with a little smile. "And does it have

to be your wagon? I have another one all ready to go. Someone just canceled."

"No, any wagon is fine. Today." Ryan didn't want Ezra to think any wagon would be fine on his trips to the future, because he needed his own narrow wagon to get through the cave. "And Ezra, could you saddle Treetop for me?"

Ryan helped Mary Elizabeth off Dolly, and Ezra brought out the other horse and wagon and parked them in the front. Then he took Dolly from Ryan and put her into a stall.

Ryan, not knowing the horse in front of him, shook the reins, and they were off. Mary Elizabeth didn't say anything during the few minutes it took to get to her house, but she wanted him to stop the wagon a few houses away. "No," he said to her. "We don't have to do that anymore. I'll take you all the way home." The horse continued, and Ryan turned the wagon around in front of the house and parked it. Then he got out, helped her to climb down from the seat, and said, "I'll see you real soon."

"You mean tomorrow?" she asked.

Ryan winked at her as he climbed back into the wagon. "I mean real soon."

Mary Elizabeth looked at him, confused, and then walked into the barn instead of the house. She's just delaying matters, thought Ryan. Well, maybe she'll stay in there until I return, and that would be perfect. He saw that their wagon was up against the side of the barn, but he didn't know if her father had taken that to work or his horse.

A few minutes later, he was back at the livery. He started to unharness the horse, but Ezra came out to stop him. "It's okay, Ryan, I'll do it. Your horse is saddled, and Dolly has her hot mash. I'll still give her more of a rub down, though."

"Thanks so much, Ezra." He handed him a silver dollar and then proceeded to the stall where Treetop was. After slipping on the bridle, he checked the cinch and climbed onto the tall horse's back. "See ya later, Ezra. Thanks!"

Treetop had a long stride, and in almost no time, they were back at Mary Elizabeth's house. He hoped she was still in the barn, but she wasn't. Climbing off the big horse, he walked him into the barn to find an empty stall. Cookie was in the stall closest to the door, and the big red stallion was at the stall farthest back. He whinnied when he saw Ryan bring in another horse. Ryan put Treetop in the stall across from Cookie and away from the big stallion, who was stamping his feet and still whinnying. He stroked Treetop's face. "Don't worry, boy. This is just temporary."

Walking resolutely to the house, he knew what he must do. When he knocked, a very surprised Mary Elizabeth answered the door. "Ryan! What are you doing here?"

"I'm here for supper!" He smiled warmly at her.

First, she put both hands to her face, and then she started to open her arms to hug him, but stopped midway, glanced over her shoulder into the house, and then finished the hug. "You were invited to supper *here*!" When he nodded, she pulled him into the house. "You've met my father; come in and meet my mother!"

Being pulled along by the hand, Ryan followed her into the kitchen. It was a medium size room with a large kitchen cookstove on one side, shelving and cabinets on one side, and a large window overlooking the street on the other side. A kitchen table sat in the center opposite the cookstove. Mary Elizabeth's mother was pulling something out of the stove.

"Mama"—she waited for her to turn around and straighten—"this is Ryan. Ryan, this is my mama."

Mrs. Mills curtsied to him. "Nice making your acquaintance, Ryan. I'm so glad you could join us for supper."

"I'm grateful to Mr. Mills for inviting me, Ma'am."

Mr. Mills walked into the room and cleared his throat. Ryan thought that he was a man used to having a presence. "Ryan, so glad you could make it. When Mary Elizabeth told me that someone had invited you for supper tonight, I hoped that you meant us! Why don't we all sit down. Cora, dear, supper is close, right?"

"Yes, dear, I'm just checking on the ribs now."

"Did someone butcher one of their cows? Usually they let me know," said Ryan.

"Oh, no. I have meat brought in every week from the city. You've been here how long now? A year? I'm surprised you don't know about that." He hesitated and then continued. "Well, admittedly, I'm the only one in town who uses them, but—"

"You'll have to give me their information—if you don't mind. I'm sure it would be cheaper than the meat that I—um, get." He sneaked a look in Mary Elizabeth's direction, and she suppressed a grin.

"Yes, I would be happy to do that."

"And in exchange for your kindness, I would be happy to share with you some of the salad that I bring in for friends and family."

"Salad?" asked Cora Mills, pulling the ribs out of the oven. "Wherever do you get salad this time of year?"

"Ryan has his sources, but they're secret, right, Ryan?"

"It's a very small supply, and I've been sworn to secrecy," said Ryan, smiling.

"Okay, no more shoptalk." Cora Mills placed a steaming plate of ribs on the table, and next to them, a plate of mashed potatoes, and finally a plate of beets. "Time to eat!" She sat down and said, "Now let's say grace."

All Ryan could focus on was the warmth of Mary Elizabeth's hand in his, and when he should do it. Now? Should he do it now before they started eating, or should he wait? He wasn't sure. It wasn't until Mr. Mills shook his hand free of Ryan's that he realized that grace was over.

As they passed the food around, Mr. Mills said, "So, Ryan. What did you do before you owned Ralston General Store?"

"Before I moved here? Well, I owned another kind of store in a larger city. I sold it because it was taking up too much of my time, and I didn't have enough time to paint."

"And he is a *great* painter, Cora!" Mr. Mills sat up straighter in his chair, if that was possible. "I have commissioned him to do a painting of me—for behind my desk at the bank."

"That's nice, dear," she said.

Ryan smiled. "I have to finish the one of Mary Elizabeth first."

"Oh, yes, of course. You'll let me know when we can start?"

"Yes, Mr. Mills. I certainly will."

"You know Edward, at the hotel, also paints. He was having some trouble getting paints, though, last time we spoke of it, which was quite some time ago."

"Yes. I get him his paints now, and he's back to painting. He's married to my grandmother—you know—Granny."

"That old woman at the hotel is your grandmother? Oh, I didn't know that." Mr. Mills stabbed at his ribs like they were going to get away from him.

Suddenly, Ryan felt like it had to be now. Now or never. It had to be now before he lost his nerve. "I have a question that I'd like to ask you, Mr. Mills."

Mr. Mills looked up from his plate with a twinkle in his eye and a smile on his lips. "I bet you're going to ask me if you can court my daughter."

Ryan, unprepared for that response, said, "Um, no, Sir, I'm already courting her. What I wanted to ask was—"

Mr. Mills dropped his fork and pounded his fist on the table. "You're *what*?"

Ryan, undaunted, said a little louder, "What I wanted to ask, Sir, is for your approval to *marry* her—that is, if it's all right with Mary Elizabeth."

As Mr. Mills looked at Mary Elizabeth—who had a beatific smile on her face—his anger faded. "Mary Elizabeth?" he said formally. "Is that all right with you?"

She glanced briefly at her father and then looked at Ryan. He wished he could keep that look forever. "Yes, Papa, it is all right with me."

"Then, Ryan—what is your last name, boy?"

"Leyton, sir."

"Then, Ryan Leyton, I officially give you permission to marry my daughter."

Cora Mills leaned over and embraced her daughter. "Oh, Mary Elizabeth. Congratulations. You won't be a spinster after all."

189

At that, Ryan, who had just taken a drink of the water in front of him, spit it all over Cora Mills, who had returned to her seat in front of him. "Oh, sorry, Mrs. Mills. I just never thought of my very beautiful Mary Elizabeth . . . "—he reached out and touched her hand —"as a spinster. She has always and only been a very lovely young woman to me." He looked at Mr. and Mrs. Mills and then at Mary Elizabeth. "And I love her."

"Well," said Mr. Mills, "there are worse reasons than that to get married. It's time to celebrate. Cora, bring out the champagne!"

Cora Mills stood up, opened one of the cabinets, took out a bottle of champagne, and handed it to Mr. Mills along with a towel. He removed the top wrapping, placed the towel over it, and gently pried the cork loose. Cora handed out wine glasses, Mr. Mills poured, and they all clinked their glasses together in celebration.

CHAPTER FORTY

ALTHOUGH MARY ELIZABETH was bursting with joy at her impending marriage to Ryan, something had started to bother her. In all the excitement about the new Red Bluff and about Ryan, and even about Bear, she had forgotten about her manuscript. Was she a writer or wasn't she? If she was, she better start writing again, or that rude woman, Miss Prosser, would be right. Before she left for the hotel, she gathered all her papers and stuck them into her handbag. Then she grabbed a quick breakfast with her mother—now that they were talking again—and walked outside. Her father had generously put Cookie into the harness already, so she didn't have to do it herself. She smiled about how everything changed once she was promised in marriage.

Climbing into the wagon, she thought about how much her life had changed in just a few short weeks. Would all this have occurred sooner had she made an effort to catch Ryan alone in his store so they could talk? That was something she would never know. When she dropped off Cookie and the wagon at the livery, it seemed like Ezra had a broader smile for her today.

Actually, everything looked brighter today. How could it not be? She was getting married! To someone that she loved! And she wouldn't be a spinster any longer! Could life possibly get any better? Yes, she thought. It could. She and Ryan could be moving to the new Red Bluff. That would be better.

Walking into the hotel, she called out, "Hi, Granny! I'm ready for work today!"

Grumbling, Granny appeared from Eliza's sitting room. "Mary Elizabeth, you were absent from work two days, not just one like you asked."

"But I got stuck in the snow!"

"No matter. I'm docking your pay two days."

It took Mary Elizabeth a minute to figure out what she had said. Docking her pay. Her pay was a penny a day. Granny was docking her two pennies. When she looked at Granny, the old woman looked irritated, so Mary Elizabeth didn't know what to do. "Um, did you want me to work today?"

"Of course I want you to work today, unless you want me to dock your pay again. Or do you not need to work anymore since you're marrying my rich grandson?" Granny looked at her, smiled, and embraced her in a big hug. "Congratulations, Mary Elizabeth. Welcome to the family!"

"Thank you, Granny! How did you know?"

"How could I not know? Ryan had to burst in on us last night after we were already in bed to tell us the good news, and first thing this morning, your father bursts in on us before we were *out* of bed! Can't a couple get any privacy around here!"

Mary Elizabeth laughed. "What would you like me to do?"

"How about starting by doing the dishes in the restaurant? Those people will be coming down any time now, and then you can wait on them. I'll do the cooking. Edward is out and about somewhere."

"Those people are still here? Sorry I missed those two days, you must have been really busy."

"They left after breakfast the first day you were gone, and they didn't return until last night. Apparently, they are stagecoach executives, trying to decide if we need one here, or if the one in the next town is enough to meet our needs. What do you think?"

Mary Elizabeth thought for a while before answering. "Well, a few weeks ago I would have said that we definitely need one here. It would have given me more opportunities to escape. But now—"

"Now that you're getting married, you mean—?"

"No, I don't mean that at all. Now that I've been to the *new* Red Bluff, I'm not so excited about taking the stage anywhere around here."

"Don't tell me that you have it, too," said Granny, shaking her head.

"Have what?"

"Future fever, like young Zack. He did tell you all the trouble he had moving there from here, right?"

"Yes, he told me, but I still think there must be a way."

"Why would you want to go to that awful place, anyway? I couldn't wait to get out of there. When I lived there, it was like I was just waiting to die. Here, I'm living my life! I feel alive!"

"Yes, but I'm still young, Granny. I could live my life *there*."

"Believe me, Mary Elizabeth, the future is not what it's cracked up to be."

193

"What do you mean?"

"All you see now are the glitter and the gloss. There are bad things there, as well."

"Zack is happy there."

"Zack is going to college and getting an education that he couldn't have received here. And his woman is there. But your man is *here*."

"We could move there *together*."

"Ryan wants to stay here. He loves it here. But if I know my grandson, and I do, if it would make you happy, he would move there *for you*. All I'm saying is, be careful what you wish for. Before you ask him to do that, spend more time there. It might make you realize how full your life could be here. But right now, the dishes need to be done. Off with you!"

While Mary Elizabeth did the dishes, she thought about what Granny had said. Spend more time there before deciding—or before asking Ryan to move back there permanently. She might as well. Next chance she had, with or without Ryan, she'd go back.

CHAPTER FORTY-ONE

WHEN SHE WALKED in the front door of the store, Ryan ran to her, picked her up in his arms, swung her around, and kissed her soundly on the lips. Bear had been sleeping, but with the commotion, he barked excitedly and jumped up on them both. Mary Elizabeth bent down and picked him up, and Ryan hugged both of them together. "He's our first child, isn't he?" He looked at her warmly.

She nodded, kissed Bear on the top of the head, and then kissed Ryan again. Ryan took Bear from her and put him on the ground. The puppy ran straight for the door and scratched. He picked the puppy back up, opened the door and let him outside, where the puppy piddled. Then Ryan let him back inside.

"What was that about?" Mary Elizabeth stood there watching with a confused look on her face.

"Good news. Josiah and Jenna already have him housebroken! Bear scratched at the door so he could go outside." Ryan smiled at her. "To what do I owe this unexpected visit? Aren't you working today?"

"I have a couple hours off before dinner, er, lunch. I

wanted to talk to you about a couple of things."

Ryan worried that she would ask him to move back to the new Red Bluff. He would, of course, if she asked it, but he really didn't want to. And since there was no way for her to get "legal" like Zack did, why would she want that, anyway? Luckily, that's not what she asked.

"You know, I wanted a horse, right?" She looked at him seriously, until he nodded. "Well, should I buy one here or, you know, *there*?"

"Here. They are much more expensive there, sometimes thousands more. You can pick one up from Ezra for less than a hundred dollars."

"Well, I definitely have that much!" She patted her handbag. "What should I get?"

"What do you want, or more specifically, what do you want it for?"

"Just regular riding around, racing with you"—she smiled at him and continued—"riding over *there*, you know. Nothing specific. I guess it would be a bonus if he pulled a wagon, but we could teach him that, right?"

"Okay, so you said, 'he.' Do you want a gelding?"

"I sure don't want a stallion! I handled Rojo okay when I rode him, but I don't want a horse that I constantly have to look out for."

"What color horse do you want?"

"Shouldn't we go see what Ezra has first before I get my heart set on a certain color?"

"It's been my experience that sometimes when you focus on exactly what you want, and feel what it would feel like to have that thing—whatever it is—sometimes it actually comes to you."

"Well, maybe in the future, but it doesn't work like that here." She put her hands on her hips. "Well, I'll try it, but it just sounds silly!"

"What color then?" asked Ryan.

"A blue roan, sixteen hands high, and nine years old. And a horse who I can ride like the wind!" She twirled around and smiled at him.

"Anything else important to you?"

"I want him to be like Bear!"

"What do you mean, 'be like Bear'?"

"You know how Bear is always excited to see me? I want a horse that's happy to see me, too. Do you think that's specific enough?"

"I think it's perfect." He kissed her.

"Can I have my typewriter now?"

"It's yours, sure." Ryan walked into the back room to get it. "Here it is, and I put some paper in there for you, too. Do you know the keys yet?"

"I still need a lot of practice, but I finished learning them all yesterday. Zack and Madison left early for school, so I worked on typing most of the day. I'm getting fast already!"

Ryan nodded. "I bet you are."

"Can I look at your coin book? Zack didn't put many ten dollar gold pieces on the list you have, and no twenty dollar gold pieces, so I thought I'd concentrate on those. I got really lucky with the other coin I found. Maybe I'll get lucky again!"

"With an attitude like that, I just bet you will! I'll give you the book, but I'd rather have you just write down what you need and leave the book here. Right on the front cover it says, *United States Coins 2014* in big letters. I really don't want it to get out. Is that okay?"

"Sure! I understand. What my father might say if he got a look at that, I don't even want to guess."

Ryan ran upstairs, got the book and a paper and pencil, and brought it halfway down the stairs. Then he ran back upstairs, grabbed her iPhone, and left it on the step beside the book. "Mary Elizabeth, here's the book, and I brought your iPhone, too. I don't really want the book out even in my back room. Too many people coming and going."

"Sure, Ryan, thank you." She climbed the steps to meet him. "What's up there?"

"Where I live. Where *we'll* live. Hope you like it." He walked past her down the stairs.

She sat down on the stair where he had handed her the book and the paper and pencil. "Can I see it sometime?"

"Of course, Mary Elizabeth. Want to see it—?" The front door opened and interrupted him. "Oh, someone's here now. Maybe later."

CHAPTER FORTY-TWO

AFTER COPYING DOWN the coins from Ryan's book, she visited the bank again. With the leftover money that Zack had given her, she bought ten twenty-dollar gold pieces. Most of them were worth less than two thousand dollars and only one of them was worth five thousand. Still, it would be a good haul. She liked this. It was like playing the future against the past and profiting from it. Her father had come in to see what she was doing, but instead of questioning her, he nodded his head, smiled, and left her alone. She wasn't even married yet, and already everything was better.

When she returned to the hotel after getting the coins from the bank, there were no customers, so she showed Granny her collection of coins. Granny looked at them and said, "I have one of those in the drawer. But they aren't on Zack's list." Picking it up, she glanced at it and then handed it to Mary Elizabeth. "I think it's the same as one of yours." Mary Elizabeth checked her list and said, "You got lucky, Granny. This one is worth more than five thousand!"

"Well, what do you know? I'm a regular thousandaire! Will you take care of it for me?"

"Sure. I'll just give it to Zack when I give him mine. He'll give you what it's worth minus ten per cent."

Granny curled into herself and pretended that she had a cane. "You mean he would take advantage of a poor old woman like me?" she said in a weak sounding voice. Then she cackled loudly and disappeared into Eliza's sitting room.

Since she hadn't given Mary Elizabeth anything to do, Mary Elizabeth checked behind the front desk, but everything was caught up. Then she walked into the restaurant, and all the tables were clean, and the dishes finished. She was free. So she pulled out her typewriter and set it up behind the front desk. After pulling out her handwritten story, she read it over and began to type. A few minutes later, the ideas were flying, and so were her fingers. The typewriter made it so much easier to write! Her hands were almost quick enough to keep up with the ideas flowing in her mind. This was so easy, she thought, she could write a hundred books!

When people started entering the hotel in the late afternoon, Mary Elizabeth put the typewriter away, and she and Granny took care of the whole supper crowd. Afterward, Granny thanked her for helping, and let her go home.

The following morning Mary Elizabeth got a surprise when she dropped off Old Cookie and the wagon at the livery. When Ezra saw her, he said, "Mary Elizabeth, I heard you were looking for a horse."

"Did you see Ryan?"

Ezra shook his head. "Nope, haven't seen him."

"What color is the horse?"

"He's a blue roan, Mary Elizabeth."

Mary Elizabeth started laughing. "Now I know you're trying to hornswoggle me, Ezra!" But when she looked at him, he looked confused and innocent.

"He's a nice horse, Mary Elizabeth. I think you'd like him."

"Save him for me, Ezra. I have to run off to work now, but I'll bring Ryan over to see him later. Okay?"

Ezra smiled. "I'll hold him for you, Miss."

Mary Elizabeth hurried off to work, and she couldn't wait until she had time off to show Ryan the new horse that Ezra thought was perfect for her. If Ryan didn't tell him, how did Ezra know she was looking for a horse, anyway? It didn't matter—he just did, and maybe Ryan was right. Maybe this horse would be exactly what she was looking for.

"What are you so all-fired excited about now?" asked Granny when she saw Mary Elizabeth skipping around.

"Ezra thinks he has a horse that I would like! I'm excited about seeing it!"

"So why didn't you look at it when you dropped your wagon off?"

"I didn't want to be late."

"Oh, piffle!" said Granny. "Go look at the dang horse! People will wonder why you're dancing around like that! They'll think you're crazy as a loon!"

"I need to have Ryan look at him, too. I can wait, Granny. I'll settle down. Promise."

"After you finish the breakfast dishes, go ahead and fetch Ryan and look at your new horse. Take as long as you need. Buying a horse is an important decision. Make sure he's a good one."

"Thanks so much, Granny."

Mary Elizabeth could hardly wait until all the customers had finished eating, so she could do the dishes and leave. When the dishes were finally finished, she said good-bye to Granny and raced down the street to get Ryan. "Ryan! Ryan!" she called, as she opened the door.

"Yes, my dearest. How wonderful to see you today," Ryan said, holding his arms open for Mary Elizabeth to come into them for a hug.

But she walked right past him toward the back door, and said, "Ezra has a horse for me to look at! Come see it with me! It's a blue roan!"

Ryan laughed. "A blue roan? That's awesome!" He reached down and scooped up Bear and followed Mary Elizabeth out the back door.

When they reached the livery and Ezra saw them, he said, "I'll go get the horse. Wait'll you see him. He's a beauty!"

A minute later he walked out with a beautiful blue roan. The horse had a black face, black legs, and black mane and tail. Mary Elizabeth thought he was gorgeous. When Ezra walked up to her, she put out her hand to touch the horse's face, and he nickered.

"See?" said Ezra. "He likes you already!"

She looked at Ryan and smiled. "He is really pretty."

"How'd you come by him, Ezra?"

"Some guy came in wanting to sell him. Said he was too much horse for him. But, Mary Elizabeth, I figured if you could ride your father's stallion, you could handle him."

"What else do you know about the horse?" asked Ryan.

"He was a race horse in his youth, but not fast enough to be a winner, so they retired him. He's been a saddle horse for several years now—came from the South.

That's why I thought of you, Mary Elizabeth. You're from the South and so is he!"

"How old is he? And about how tall do you think he is?" Ryan walked around the horse looking at it from all angles.

"He's eight years old now, and will turn nine later this year. And he's sixteen one," said Ezra.

"Oh, Ryan, he's wonderful!" said Mary Elizabeth, barely paying any attention to the conversation between the two men.

"How much do you want for him, Ezra?" asked Ryan.

"I'll tell you what, Ryan. I don't need another horse. I have plenty. I'll sell him to you for what I paid. But he's a great horse, and he was expensive. Forty dollars."

Ryan nodded and asked, "You checked to make sure he's sound, right?"

"Oh, he's definitely sound. All the way around." Ezra motioned toward the horse's four legs. "I checked for hot spots, everything. He's good. If not, I'll buy him back. You don't have to worry about buying a lame horse from me."

Ryan smiled at him while Mary Elizabeth continued to stroke the horse. "Sweety? Everything sounds good. You still want him?"

"Oh, he's mine already, Ryan. He's mine already!" She hugged the horse's neck and smiled at Ryan.

CHAPTER FORTY-THREE

THAT AFTERNOON, MARY Elizabeth was so distracted thinking about her new horse that she didn't get any writing done. She just looked about dreamily until Granny told her that she looked unconscious. After the supper crowd left, she walked to the livery and went to visit her new horse in his stall at the back while Ezra got Cookie and her wagon ready. "What a good boy you are," she crooned to the horse, who nickered back at her in response.

"Here you go, Mary Elizabeth. When are you going to take him home?"

"Well, you know Ryan and I are getting married." She looked at Ezra with a shy smile.

"Yes, I heard. Congratulations to the both of you."

"And Ryan keeps his horse here—and Dolly—so I was thinking instead of taking him home and having him get used to it there, that I should just leave him here. And maybe after we're married I could talk Ryan into a corral and shelter so I could keep him there!"

"Ah, trying to horn in on my business, huh?" asked Ezra.

Shocked, Mary Elizabeth lost her smile. "Oh, no, Ezra, I'm sorry, it's just—"

"Now I'm hornswoggling you, Mary Elizabeth. Two horses will not make a difference to me!"

"Oh, okay."

Ezra reached out his hand and stroked the black face. "He is a pretty boy. What are you going to name him?"

Her eyes popped open. "What did the man who sold him to you call him?"

"He didn't say, and he's already left town. You can name him anything you want."

She looked at the big horse, tilted her head one way then the other, and whispered to the horse, "What do you think of Blue?" The horse picked his head up and then back down again, and Mary Elizabeth said, "I think that's a yes, don't you, Ezra?" When Ezra nodded, she said, "His name is Blue." Then she stroked the horse again, whispered good-bye, and walked out front to drive the wagon home.

It surprised Mary Elizabeth how well she was getting along with her parents now. No more cruel comments about spring chickens, and no more nasty comments accusing Ryan of being a mudsill. Now that her father had met him and talked to him, and even wanted to buy a *painting* from him, everything was different. And her parents now considered her their "almost married" daughter instead of their spinster daughter—which took a lot of pressure off her. Almost married was practically as good as being married. And that was good enough for her.

She and Ryan hadn't even talked about setting a date yet. Mary Elizabeth hoped that he wasn't one of those men who wanted an extended engagement so he could get used to the idea of getting married. But he didn't seem to be like that. When he had asked her father for her hand in marriage, it surprised her as much as it surprised her father. It still tickled her when she thought about when Ryan said that he had already been courting her—and the look on her father's face. Although Ryan appeared to be very calm and easy-going, he wasn't afraid to stand up to her father. And she was very grateful for that. If she would marry a man who constantly bowed to her father's every whim, it wouldn't be much better for Mary Elizabeth than living at home with her father. Ryan was perfect for her! But she did wonder about how soon they'd get married, and she thought she'd ask him next time she saw him.

The following morning when Mary Elizabeth went in to work—after saying hallo to Blue—she found Granny at the front desk. "Hello, child. It looks like we're losing all of our guests this afternoon."

"This afternoon?"

"The stagecoach executives are having a big meeting this morning with men from businesses all over town. They want to make sure that the town can handle the new influx of people. You know what *influx* means?" she asked.

"I went to college, Granny."

"Oh! Well, I wasn't sure if it was a word yet—because *I* never went to college!"

"I thought everyone in *your* time went to college."

"Not everyone. *I* didn't. Most kids nowadays do, though. It's more difficult getting a job if you don't. Anyway, what was I saying? You distracted me. Oh, yes, the meeting. That's where Edward was the other day. They consulted him first because they figured that the hotel would be the first business to feel the increase in patronage. People will stay here between other stops on the stage. So Edward had to agree to expand the hotel. Won't Eliza and Samuel be surprised when they find out!"

"Wow. Will they be mad?"

"At more business? I doubt it."

"When are they coming home, anyway?"

"Not until they find their son. No one knows how long that will take. They don't even know where he is, although they know he disappeared in Virginia."

"Maybe they won't find him at all. Maybe he is dead." Mary Elizabeth dusted the counter with a rag from behind the desk.

"He died in Red Bluff. Jenna found that out on the internet when she was checking out Josiah."

"Oh, that's right. Jenna told me that when Ryan and I ate dinner there."

"Anyway, after the stagecoach crew have breakfast and we clean up, then you and I need to make sandwiches for them to take back with them. They're leaving right after the meeting."

"They won't get there till dark," said Mary Elizabeth, concerned.

"So? The road is clear. No bandits that we know of. What are you concerned for? I didn't realize you were a fraidy-cat."

"At first I am, until I'm comfortable around something. When Ryan first took me over *there*, we stepped out of the cave, and a jet flew over! I cowered down and covered my head skeery that it would hit me. I thought if the whole new world was like that then I would hate it. But I got over it and learned to embrace

207

all the new and somewhat frightening things there."

"And now you want to move there." Granny shook her head as she looked at Mary Elizabeth.

"Well, yeah, I think I do. But I'm going back there again like you said."

"When?" asked Granny.

"I don't know. Ryan can't go until Sunday."

"Didn't my great-granddaughter tell you that you could visit anytime?"

"Yes, she did say that. And she said with or without Ryan. But if Madison and Zack aren't home, and Ryan doesn't come with me, then how could I get anywhere?"

"There is something called a taxicab. You use a phone to call them up, tell them where you want to go, they pick you up, take you, and then you pay them. Do you have money?"

"Yes, and I have a phone, too."

"You have a phone? What would you need with a phone?"

Shrugging, Mary Elizabeth said, "Madison gave it to me. I can use it when I'm there—and if we move there."

Granny frowned and shook her head. "Girl, you need to go there tomorrow. Get this new world stuff out of your head."

"Ryan goes on Sundays, though."

"You need to go alone. And don't ride that new horse of yours, ride Dolly. She knows the way there and home so you won't get lost."

"Why alone?"

"To see what it's like by yourself. That will give you a taste of the new world. Yes, it has ice cream, and fancy restaurants, but there are dark things, too. What I'd like you to do when you get there is to read the newspaper."

Mary Elizabeth laughed. "Why would I want to do that? I won't know any of the people getting married or having babies."

"Newspapers have changed. That's still in there, but after that, it's mostly bad news. And reading the newspaper is how you'll learn of the dark things."

"Okay. I'll do that then."

"After we finish making the sandwiches, I want you to go over and see my grandson and tell him you're going. I don't want him to be mad at me for sending you over there alone if you don't tell him first. But don't let him go with you. It will be a completely different experience for you if you're there alone."

CHAPTER FORTY-FOUR

RYAN WAS IN the back working on a painting, but he looked over his shoulder at the half-finished painting of Mary Elizabeth. He had gone as far as he could with the pictures he had taken. What he really needed was for her to sit for him again. Next time he saw her, he'd have to ask her about that. And now with the proposed stagecoach coming in, he'd have even less time to paint. Unless—

The front door opened and Mary Elizabeth walked in with a big smile on her face. "Hi, Ryan!" She came over to him and hugged him while he was sitting in the chair. "Where's my painting? Are you finished with it?" she asked excitedly.

When Ryan motioned over his shoulder, he heard Mary Elizabeth moan. "Sorry. I was going to ask you— next time you have a day off, would you mind sitting for me again so I can finish?"

"No, I don't mind, but it can't be the next day off, because that is tomorrow."

"Oh, that would be perfect."

She shook her head. "Sorry, Ryan. I'm going to *town*."

"I'm going Sunday. You can go with me then. And sit for me tomorrow. It will be perfect." Ryan turned back to his painting like it was all decided. He touched up the sky with the blue that he had just mixed.

"No, I'm sorry, Ryan. I'm going to town *alone*. Granny said it would be a different experience for me if I'm alone."

"But if Madison and Zack aren't home, then you can't get anywhere. If you wait until Sunday, I can take you anywhere you want to go." When she made an unidentifiable sound in her throat, he said, "No! You can't drive my car!"

Mary Elizabeth laughed. "I didn't think I could. But Granny said there's something called a taxicar that will take me anywhere I want to go."

"Taxicab. True. But why do you want to go without me?" He dabbed on another bit of blue paint. "You don't have another guy there, do you?" He looked at her accusingly.

She laughed, and then he laughed. "No, no other guy. But, Ryan, you know that I'm interested in moving there —even though Zack and Madison told me why I can't ever be 'legal,' and Granny told me that it was a bad idea, regardless. I just want to see for myself, that's all. And Granny wants me to be sure to read a newspaper."

"Read a newspaper? Why?"

"Because of all the bad news! She says it's not like the newspapers here."

"She's got that right. It *is* all bad news. I stopped watching the news years ago. Too depressing." Ryan stood up, frowned, put his hands on her shoulders, and looked into her eyes. "Okay, if you really want to go, go ahead. But I don't think you should ride your new horse

211

—."

"Blue, I named him Blue."

"Oh, good name! I know you're eager to ride him, but I don't think you should ride Blue over there. Ask Granny if you can ride Dolly—she knows the way."

"Granny already suggested that." She hesitated, looked around, and then said, "Ryan, where's Bear?"

"Oh! Bear! When I went to that meeting earlier—did you hear about it? The stagecoach, I mean—anyway, I couldn't bring Bear so I dropped him off next door. Nick is watching him for me."

"Yes, I heard about the stagecoach. Sounds like a big deal for Red Bluff."

"It's going to change everything, really."

"It might change it so much that you'll want to move to *town* with me."

He gave her a dirty look and returned to the painting. "Mary Elizabeth, I chose to move *here*. I really like it here. Sure, the stagecoach coming to town will change things, but they won't change so much that I'd rather be *there* than here. If you insist that you want to move there, then we'll talk about it. Okay?"

She nodded. "Ryan, we also need to talk about—"

The front door opened and in rushed Bear, jumping all over her and licking her face and hands when she kneeled down. Nick followed him in and said, "Thought you might like this guy back. He's been a bundle of fun, but it's time for him to return to his, um, parents! See ya later, guys!"

"Thanks, Nick! I appreciate it. Bye!"

"Well, I better get home for supper. Would you like to join us tonight, Ryan? I'm sure it will be okay."

"No thank you. I want to get this painting finished.

What time are you going tomorrow?"

"Early."

"Will you stop by here when you come home, so I know that you've safely returned?"

"Sure, Ryan." She stood above him and kissed the top of his head. "I'll see you tomorrow." Then she kneeled down again and tried to kiss the top of Bear's head while he tried to lick her face. "I'll see *you* tomorrow, too!" Then she stood up and walked out the back door, trying to keep Bear from following her out.

Ryan watched as she walked out and smiled. She was his. Almost. Oh, he had forgotten that he wanted to talk to her about setting a wedding date. He wasn't sure how it worked in the nineteenth century, but he hoped that her father wouldn't want her to have a long engagement. He also hoped that *she* didn't want a long engagement. Now that he had made up his mind to marry, he just wanted it to be over—get married and get on with living —*together*.

CHAPTER FORTY-FIVE

MARY ELIZABETH HAD a difficult time sleeping that night. Although she had been *there* before—even ridden over there by herself—this time felt new to her, like she was checking out the real estate before buying. She knew in her heart that she would want to stay there, live there, raise a family there. Ryan had said that if she for sure wanted to move there, then they would talk about it— which meant he was willing to listen to her point of view. He could have just said no, but she didn't think Ryan was like that. Granny had said she thought that he would move back there if she wanted to. She did. She really wanted to move there. And there wasn't anything that she could think of that would change her mind. Of course, it *was* a different world there. Mary Elizabeth knew that she didn't know everything there was to know about the place. But that's why she was riding out there —to find out more. What she *expected*, though, was to love every single thing she would learn about the place.

When the rooster crowed, she opened her eyes, stretched, got up, and dressed. Her parents would not know that she wasn't working today. There was no way she could tell them, anyway! Now that they were content with her impending nuptials, they had no reason to check on her. That was not something she was going to worry about. This trip was going to be—awesome—as Ryan puts it, and she was going to enjoy every minute while she was there. And she hoped that when she returned and talked to Ryan about how much she wanted to move there, that he would agree, and then they would make their plans on moving to the twenty-first century after their marriage.

After a quick breakfast, Mary Elizabeth walked outside to find that, although it was Saturday, her father had already hooked Cookie up to the wagon for her. When she peeked into the barn, Rojo was still there. He had gotten up intentionally just to help her out. She smiled. Maybe Ryan moved here to the old Red Bluff in order for him to meet *her* and marry her. And then he could return. With her—as his wife.

She drove into town, dropped Cookie and the wagon off at the livery, and picked up Dolly, who Ezra had already saddled for her because she had mentioned it to him the previous day. Before she left, though, she stopped to see Blue, who nuzzled her as she stroked his neck. Then she rode out of town, straining to see in the window of Ralston General Store and hoping to see Ryan there. But he wasn't, and she turned off at the side trail and rode through the cave and out the other side. As she emerged, she heard another jet going by and although she cowered momentarily, it didn't bother her like before. Not a big deal, she thought, I could get used to that. Letting Dolly pick her way down the trace, they soon came to the main trail and turned off toward the ranch. Not long after that, they arrived at the gates.

Dolly was so good that Mary Elizabeth could open them from the saddle, and once on the other side, latch them up again. And then they were at the barn. She took Dolly's bridle off, made sure she had water, and strolled into the driveway feeling like someone special.

Zack's and Madison's cars were both there, so she knocked on the door. Madison opened the door with a huge smile and hugged her. "Mary Elizabeth! You came!" Then she peered out the door past Mary Elizabeth. "Is Ryan here?"

"No, Granny thought I should come on my own."

"Well, I told you that you're welcome here, and you are, but Zack and I are leaving soon. We're meeting some friends and going up into the mountains for lunch. Oh! You could come with us!"

"Thanks, Madison, but I need to stay here. Granny said that I could take a taxicab anywhere I wanted to go."

"You can! I can leave the number for you, or you can look it up on the internet. Your laptop is still here, isn't it?"

"Yes, I left it, the iPod, and the iPad." She reached into her handbag and pulled something out. "But I brought my iPhone!"

Madison laughed. "You can call on that. Did Zack show you how?"

"Yes, but I've probably forgotten. Is he here now? I brought some more coins for him."

"Zack! Mary Elizabeth is here!"

Mary Elizabeth heard in the background, "Be right there."

"I think he's getting dressed," said Madison. "We were up late last night."

"Here I am!" Zack came running out. "I have the rest of your money from those other coins, Mary Elizabeth."

"And I have some more for you, Zack." She reached into her handbag, pulled out the coins, and began searching through them. "Ah, here it is. This one is from Granny, and she didn't think you should charge her!"

Zack laughed and looked at Granny's coin and then the others. "Granny's coin and this coin are quite valuable, and these others are right around two thousand each."

"That's about what I figured," said Mary Elizabeth.

"I'll go get the other money for you. Did Madison tell you we were leaving for the day?"

"Yeah, that's okay. Granny told me that I should be here on my own before I decide about the place."

"You still have your heart set on living here even though you can't be legal, huh? That's a tough one. I'll be right back."

Zack disappeared down the hallway, and Mary Elizabeth sat down on the couch. "Hey, Mary Elizabeth," Zack called. "Come in here." She walked into the hallway and turned toward Zack and Madison's bedroom, and then heard Zack say, "No, in here." He was in the room where she had slept before. "I wanted to give you the rest of the money, but you need to leave most of it here, so I'm putting it in this drawer. How much do you think you need today?"

"Why can't I just take it all with me? I don't understand."

"It's not safe. This isn't like small town Red Bluff. Strangers see you with this much money and they might try to steal it from you. How about two hundred dollars?"

217

"Well, I probably don't need that much today, but it won't hurt to take it. Maybe I'll find some other electronic thing to buy!"

"Okay." Zack handed her two hundred dollars in twenties. "I'm putting the rest of the money here. I got five hundred in nineteenth-century money—I thought that would be enough for now, but if you want more, I can trade in the other money for you—and the rest in twenty-first-century money." He pointed to the drawer. "It's right in here. Leave it until before you go home, okay? It would be better to leave it until Ryan comes tomorrow. He's still coming tomorrow, right?"

"Yes, he is."

"Zack? You ready?"

"I sure am, Hon. Be right there." He looked at Mary Elizabeth. "Anything else?"

"Oh, yeah! Can you show me again how to use the iPhone?"

After Zack showed her how to use it, Madison walked into the room and gave her a piece of paper with the taxicab's number and the address of Jenna's ranch on it. Then they both said good-bye and left Mary Elizabeth all alone in the big house.

CHAPTER FORTY-SIX

RYAN WAS UPSTAIRS when Mary Elizabeth rode by. Although he waved madly to her from the window, he couldn't get it open in time. And she was only looking at the downstairs windows. It didn't matter. He'd see her later when she returned. It was a beautiful day out, and he hoped beautiful in the new Red Bluff, too. He didn't need her frantic father to pay him a visit again. And he didn't want to ride over there when he was going the next day. Of course, if she *needed* him to, he would go in a minute. Ryan knew that he would do anything for that woman.

Well, maybe not. The more he thought about her wanting to move there, the more he didn't like it. She'd never be legal—that just couldn't happen. Zack got lucky that Kat could do that for him. But it was a one time thing, never to happen again. If she couldn't be legal, it would be a constant headache for them. She couldn't drive, that was a given. What could she do? If all she wanted was to play with the electronics, he already had one of those small solar charging devices, so she could play here. And they would still go over there at least once a week. No, he didn't want to move there, and if she insisted on it, then they would have to have words about it. And the words wouldn't be nice.

For the first time with *her*, maybe the first time with *any woman*, he was determined not to go along with this. Usually he was so enamored that he did anything the woman wanted him to do, and he did it with a smile. How contradictory he thought that Mary Elizabeth was the first and only woman he had ever been in love with, and she was the only woman that he wasn't going to let push him around. Why would something like that be? Is it that the other women he knew were only temporary, and this one was permanent? He could put up with something like that on a temporary basis, but not a permanent basis—was that it?

Whatever it was, he didn't understand it, but he felt it strongly enough. If he had to, he would call off the wedding. That would make her come to her senses. And what if it didn't? What would he do then? *If* and when that happened, he would deal with it then. He hoped it wouldn't happen, but Mary Elizabeth was a strong woman with a mind of her own. That's one of the reasons that he liked her. So if he liked her for it, he couldn't be angry at her for acting like that. But he could be upset that she didn't listen to reason about the impossibilities of living in the new Red Bluff.

Maybe Granny had it right about making her read the newspaper. What else could be more negative, more depressing than a newspaper? If she does read it like Granny asked—and he thought she would—then she would get a taste of the *real* Red Bluff. And it might change her mind. He sincerely hoped that it would. Calling off the wedding was the very last thing in the world that he wanted to do.

Bear whined, and Ryan reached down to pet him. "Can you wait a few more minutes?" Bear licked him in response.

"Hey! When you going to open?" shouted a voice from downstairs that Ryan recognized as Mr. Smythe from the bank.

"Sorry, Mr. Smythe, come on in. Be down in a minute."

Mr. Smythe didn't work on Saturdays, so he would be downstairs in his jeans wanting to buy building supplies. Ryan finished his chores upstairs and climbed down the stairs, followed by Bear. "Just a minute more, Mr. Smythe." He let the puppy out the back door, waited for him, and then let him back in. Bear started licking his food dish, and Ryan wandered up to the front to take Mr. Smythe's money for the purchases he made. After Mr. Smythe left, Ryan walked around the store with a tape measure trying to figure out where to put the new shelves. The stagecoach executives insisted that he offer more products than he now carried. When they had stopped in, none of them found the disguised cooler that he kept produce in. What would they have thought of that, he wondered.

When he finished measuring for the shelves, he put a note by the cash box that he was out back. Then he walked out there and measured the back lot. He knew once Mary Elizabeth moved in with him that she would probably want her horse there close to her. Might as well surprise her with a corral before she had a chance to ask. Maybe that would make her want to stay. He'd have to ask Nick to help him build it. Although he could do it himself, but it would take a lot longer.

Oh, a composting toilet! He had forgotten about that. Mary Elizabeth would definitely love one of those. That would have to be added to the list of lumber to get for the shelves and the corral. Where would he put it? Down here so patrons could use it and ask questions that he couldn't answer? Or upstairs where no one else would see it? But he'd have to remove the outhouse because of the corral. What about the hole where the outhouse was? What was to be done about that? He wouldn't want the horses to fall into it. Maybe Josiah would know.

CHAPTER FORTY-SEVEN

IT WAS STRANGE being alone in the house, but she had things to do, and she would begin them immediately. First, she took out her laptop—she'd be so glad to get it home, but that wouldn't happen until she moved in with Ryan, whenever that was—and she clicked the google button. She didn't know what google meant, but that's what Zack had showed her to do. Then she typed in "Mary Elizabeth Leyton books" in the search box. The idea had come to her when Granny reminded her about Jenna finding out that Eliza's son was still alive. So certainly if you could find out someone was still alive, you could find out if someone had published a book.

She waited. Nothing happened. The picture on the screen stared back at her with "Mary Elizabeth Leyton books" not moving at all. There must be something she was missing. It didn't work this way when Zack showed her how to do it. Then the screen had immediately jumped to a list of possibilities. Looking at the keyboard, she studied the keys and found it! It was the rectangular key on the right-hand side that said "RETURN enter" on it. She pressed it and got a list, but nothing on it that pertained to her. Nobody named Mary Elizabeth Leyton had written any books. At least it didn't look that way. On the list were items about "books" and "Leyton" and even "Elizabeth" and "Mary" but nothing with all of those words together.

Feeling devastated, she blinked back the tears and wanted to call Ryan but knew that she couldn't reach him where he was, more than a hundred years in the past. And Madison and Zack were off on their own adventure. Having no one to turn to, she gathered herself together and closed the lid on the laptop. Okay, so she knew before she looked that this was a possibility. That awful Miss Prosser was right. Mary Elizabeth was not a writer. But if she wasn't a writer, then what was she? There was one thing she was certain about: she was not the kind of woman who could possibly be happy *just* being a wife. No, that was definitely not for her. She had a life to live, and being a wife was not enough life for her. Well, if she wasn't a writer—the thought bothered her more than she wanted to face—then she would find something else. Maybe Ryan could teach her to paint. Or something.

Taking out her iPhone, she grabbed the paper where Madison had written the telephone number for the taxicab. She was just about to tap out the number when a new idea occurred to her. Leaving the iPhone where it was, she ran back over to the laptop, opened the lid, impatiently waited for the screen to clear, and then she typed in "Mary Elizabeth Mills books." And a list of the books that she had written and that had been published by John Wiley & Sons appeared in front of her. She took a deep breath—she was a writer after all. Closing the lid with a slight smile on her face, she felt better again. What did it mean? Was she not going to marry Ryan after all? Was she going to end up a spinster? The idea frightened her. A realization hit her. She'd rather be a wife *with* Ryan than a writer without him.

Frowning, she picked up the paper and the iPhone again, tapped out the number, and asked for a taxicab. When they asked for her address, she read them the address that Madison had written on the paper. She stuck the paper in her handbag and thought, thank you, Madison. If Madison hadn't done that, Mary Elizabeth would have had no idea what the address was. After she called, she returned to the bedroom and opened the drawer to get the money that Zack put in there—it was hers, after all, and she was a big girl completely capable of handling her own money. She appreciated Zack's concern, but it seemed silly to her. But then, she heard the taxicab out front honking, so she quickly closed the drawer without taking the money and hurried out.

"Where to, Miss?" The taxicab driver turned around to look at her.

"Oh!" She realized that she hadn't thought this through. Although she knew she wanted to go *somewhere*, she hadn't really considered *where*. "I—I don't know. I guess I want to go somewhere I can buy a newspaper."

The driver pulled out into the street. "Lady, you can get a newspaper at any grocery store or on half the corners in town. You're going to have to be more specific."

That flustered her. His voice was curt and impatient. "Sir, I'm new to town. Can't you help me out here?"

"Oh, Lady! I don't know! How about the friggin' bookstore—they'll have newspapers and a map of the city. How 'bout that?"

"Perfect, thank you."

In less than fifteen minutes, he had dropped her off at the bookstore, and she had paid him and gave him a small tip. When she entered the bookstore, she looked around and smiled at the rows and rows of books. Instead of asking where the newspapers were, she decided to stroll around and find them herself. When she found them, she was delighted. Not only did they have the Red Bluff newspaper, but they had a Denver newspaper, a Chicago newspaper, and a New York City newspaper! After grabbing the local paper and the Denver paper, she found the nonfiction section and looked for the coin book that Ryan had. She grabbed a copy of that and walked up front to pay.

Taking out the stack of twenty dollar bills, she paid the man and put the rest of the money back into her handbag. He handed her the bag with her purchases in it. As she walked out, she saw two young men give her a funny look, so she glanced down to see if she had a spot on her clothes or anything. No, everything looked fine. And she was wearing a skirt and blouse that she had bought at the thrift store, so she would fit in the twenty-first century better. On her first visit to the new Red Bluff, she had realized that styles had changed. A lot.

Looking around, she thought she recognized some of the stores so she continued walking up the street. There it was! The thrift store! When she walked in, she glanced again at the skirts and blouses, but didn't see anything she liked. And she wouldn't be bringing her mother another dish this trip. So she wandered around until she found the backpacks and other traveling cases. She picked one out that her father wouldn't consider out of place, and she bought it.

CHAPTER FORTY-EIGHT

THIS WAS SO much fun! Mary Elizabeth was so glad that Granny had suggested coming to town alone! What would she do now? She looked across the street and then looked up one way and down the other. Hesitating, she heard someone say, "Hey, lady!" It was one of those young men, and he had a big smile on his face. People were certainly friendly here! Another reason to love the place. He waved at her, and she turned toward him and smiled. Suddenly someone rammed into her from behind, sending her to her hands and knees. It hurt. When she picked up her head to see what had happened, she saw the other young man running away from her with her handbag in his hands.

She couldn't stand up. Her hands were shredded and bloody from the pavement, and her knees hurt. Although she wasn't sure, she thought her knees might be scraped, too. Crawling to the side of the building, she leaned against it, clutching her purchases in her hand and drawing her knees up. Blood seeped through her skirt where her knees were. So they *were* scraped. She felt light-headed and like her head was filled with cotton. She didn't think she could get her arms and legs to move. They felt stuck. And she felt alone. Terribly alone.

What surprised her most was all the people who walked by without acknowledging her. Did things like this happen so often around here that no one paid it any attention? Or did it happen so rarely that no one knew what to do? Instinctively, she put her head against her knees and felt better. Physically, she felt better. Emotionally, all she wanted to do was crawl into bed, curl up in a ball, and sleep until the last horrible memory of this had faded away. If she had one thing to be grateful for, though, it was that she had left the rest of the money at home.

How was she going to get back to Madison's now? The paper with her address had been in the handbag. And the money! How would she pay a taxicab to take her back there? Tears flooded her eyes and dropped onto her torn and bloody skirt. People came in and out of the thrift store, and no one said a word to her. They just left her there wrapped up in her own misery. She didn't know how long she had leaned against that wall—maybe hours—when someone stepped out of the store, looked at her, and said, "Oh, no! Are you okay? What happened?" It was the woman in the store who she had bought the traveling bag from.

The question made her break into tears again. "Those men! They knocked me down and stole my handbag!"

"Do you have someone to call? Oh, I guess not, or you would have. Was your phone in your handbag, too?" The woman kneeled down to talk to Mary Elizabeth.

She nodded, feeling even more horrible about losing the phone, and then she looked up. "No! I left it on the dresser! How am I going to get home?"

The woman put her hand on Mary Elizabeth's shoulder. "I'm off now. I can take you home. Come on, my car is down there." She helped Mary Elizabeth stand up and walked her to her car, opening the door for her. When they were both settled into the car, she asked, "Okay, where do you live?"

Mary Elizabeth started crying again. "I don't know! I'm from out of town staying with a friend, and her address was in the handbag, too. What am I going to do?"

The woman comforted her and said, "Did you see the address?" Mary Elizabeth nodded. "Try to remember just the street name. "

She thought for a moment and sighed, "It was Wildview Road. I'm sure of it."

"Good. It's right down here, isn't it?" The woman pointed behind her, and Mary Elizabeth nodded.

"Yes, it's at the end of the street, and there are horses there."

The woman drove her all the way, and when Mary Elizabeth saw the house, she said, "Yes! That's it! That's it!" The car pulled into the driveway, and Mary Elizabeth said, "Thank you so much. Everybody else just walked by. Thank you for stopping and then taking the time to take me home. I appreciate it."

"They probably thought you were just homeless or something. Those poor homeless people are practically invisible. But I recognized you from when you came in. Anyway, you're home now. I'm sorry about what happened. Good luck to you."

Mary Elizabeth closed the door of the car, waved as it drove away, and then walked into the house. She went straight into her bedroom, climbed into bed, curled up into a ball, and fell asleep. Some time later, she heard Zack and Madison come in the house, laughing. Then, Madison poked her head in the door, saw Mary Elizabeth's tear-stained face, and said, "Zack! Zack! Go get Ryan! Now!"

CHAPTER FORTY-NINE

IT HAD BEEN a long day. He had felt uneasy all day long and couldn't shake a niggling feeling that something had happened to Mary Elizabeth. That was silly, he thought. What trouble could she get into buying a newspaper? And Madison and Zack would be there for her. Wouldn't they? What if they had other plans for the day, and she was left all alone? She was going to take a taxi. But she doesn't know the city at all. What if the driver took her to the other side of town and left her or something? Oh, stop it, Ryan, he told himself. You have no reason to think anything bad happened to her. She's fine and she will be riding into town at any time. He looked out the window again.

There, in the distance, a horse. See, she's coming home now. Wait. It wasn't Mary Elizabeth, it was Zack. He rode bareback, trotted up to the store's hitching post, slid off the horse's back, and without even tying the horse, Zack ran into the store. It happened too fast for Ryan to realize what was going on. But when Zack came running through the door with a look of panic on his face, Ryan went weak in the knees and had to hang onto

231

the counter.

"Ryan! Something's happened to Mary Elizabeth! You need to come back with me. Now!"

"What happened?" He grabbed Zack's shoulders. "Tell me what happened?"

"I don't know, Ryan. She was on the bed crying when we got home, and she wouldn't get up. Madison told me to get you."

"Zack, don't wait for me. I have to get my horse from the livery. Can you take the puppy next door to Nick and ask him to keep it for me? Then go home and tell Mary Elizabeth that I'll be right there! Thanks, Zack!" He saw Zack kneel down and pick up the puppy, and then he raced out the back door, down the street and into the livery.

He quickly brushed and saddled Treetop, and trotted him down the street and toward the side trail that led to the cave. They walked through the cave and down the path to the main trail; then Ryan urged Treetop faster. He took off in a canter and when Ryan urged him again, he broke into a dead run. A few minutes later, they reached the gates and went through them easily. Soon, Treetop was in the barn eating hay.

Ryan ran into the house without knocking, turned down the hallway and into the bedroom. Madison sat on the bed holding Mary Elizabeth's hand. "Ah, Ryan, you're here. Good. She needs you." Madison stood up and left the room.

"Mary Elizabeth, what happened? Are you okay?" When he took her hand and felt the bandages on it, he frowned. Then he sat on the bed beside her and touched her cheek. The tear stains on her face were unmistakable.

"They knocked me down and took my handbag!" With that one sentence, she started crying again and couldn't speak for several minutes. When she recovered herself, she told him the whole story from catching the cab to the boys knocking her down and how she sat there for hours until that kind woman had come out. "And I'm never coming back here, Ryan. Never!"

He kissed her hand gently. "Mary Elizabeth, you know what they say when you fall off a horse. You have to get right back on."

"Horses are different. They have kind hearts—most of them, anyway. But the people here—"

The tears came again and increased to deep sobs, and all Ryan could do was hold her and murmur, "There there, it will be all right. I'm here now. If you don't want to return here, you don't have to. You're fine now."

They stayed there like that for several minutes, until Mary Elizabeth leaned back and said, "Would you take me home?"

"Yes, of course. Are you ready to go now?"

When she stood up and he saw the torn skirt and bloody splotches, he said, "Let me see."

She shook her head. "No. You can't see my knees. I know girls here show their knees, but I'm not going to show you."

Ryan smiled. "Well, at least you still have your old spunk!" He motioned toward the bloody skirt, and his smile faded. "I just want to make sure you're all right."

"Madison cleaned and bandaged both knees. And she gave me this."

Mary Elizabeth picked up a tube of antibiotic oint-ment on the nightstand and held it up for Ryan to see. Ryan took it and slipped it into his pocket. Then he put his hand on her back to lead her out of the room.

Madison and Zack were in the living room, talking. They looked up when Ryan and Mary Elizabeth came out.

"We're going home now. Thank you for everything you did. Zack, thanks for coming to get me."

"Thank you, Madison, Zack, for everything," said Mary Elizabeth in a small voice.

Zack stood up. "Did you get the money?"

"No," said Mary Elizabeth. "And you can change all the twenty-first-century money into nineteenth-century money for me, because I'm never coming back here. Not ever."

Ryan put his hand under her chin so she'd look at him. "Mary Elizabeth, you might want to buy another iPod or something."

"Oh, okay," she whispered.

"Zack, give me the old money and keep the new money here, if you don't mind." Ryan put his arms around Mary Elizabeth while they waited.

Zack walked into the bedroom, got the money, and returned. "Here it is. Do you want me to count it out for you?"

"No need, Zack. If we can't trust you, who can we trust?" Ryan said, and Mary Elizabeth, still in his arms, nodded.

After getting the money from Zack, Ryan and Mary Elizabeth walked out to the barn. When she saw Ryan's big red horse, she asked, "You borrowed Rojo from my father?"

"No, this is Treetop; he's *my* horse."

"He's a beauty," she said, stroking the tall horse's face.

Ryan took Dolly out of her stall, checked the cinch,

put on the bridle, and helped Mary Elizabeth up into the saddle. Then he climbed onto Treetop's back. "Let's go."

Mary Elizabeth was fine until they left the gates and the ranch behind. Then she kept looking over her shoulder and jumping at unexpected noises.

"Mary Elizabeth, I'm right here. Nothing is going to happen to you. You're safe with me. Okay?"

She nodded. "Okay."

But she didn't stop looking around and tensing at every bird, every breeze, every rustle of brush. Ryan wondered if she'd continue to be this way after they returned to the nineteenth century. The answer came as they emerged out of the tunnel. When a hawk flew directly overhead, the sound of its big wings beating against the air, Mary Elizabeth shrank down. His mouth tightened at her response. He wondered how long it would take for her to get over this.

They came to the main trail a minute later, and Mary Elizabeth stopped. "What's wrong?" asked Ryan. "Come on, I'll ride you home and take Dolly back myself."

She slowly shook her head and tears dropped from her eyes. "I'm not going home."

CHAPTER FIFTY

"What do you mean? You *have* to go home! Your parents will have a fit if you don't come home!"

She shook her head again. "I'm not going home. I don't care. I can't let them see me like this"—she looked down at her torn, bloody skirt—"or they'll ask questions that I'm not up to answering. So I'm just not going."

"You can't come to *my* house! We're not married yet. Your father might shoot me!" said Ryan.

"Do you think Jenna and Josiah would let me stay there?"

He turned his horse the opposite direction from town. "There's only one way to find out. Come on." Ryan hoped that Jenna and Josiah would say "no," but he knew that wasn't going to happen. Of course they would say yes, and even if there was a slight doubt, once they saw her disheveled condition, they would definitely say yes. And she did look awful. His beautiful Mary Elizabeth had tear stains on her face, bandages on her hands, and a ragged skirt that begged for an explanation. Truth was, he couldn't blame her for not wanting to go home.

Jenna saw them through the window and opened the

door. She took one look at Mary Elizabeth and said, "What happened to you? Are you okay? Come on in!" When Jet sniffed at Mary Elizabeth, Jenna said, "Jet! Leave her alone! Go outside for a while."

When Mary Elizabeth finished the story, she looked at Jenna through tear-stained eyes and said, "Could I maybe stay here tonight? I can't face my parents, yet."

Jenna hugged her. "Of course you can stay here! You don't need to ask! We'll move the crib into our room, and you can have that bedroom all to yourself."

"I don't want to be any bother."

"You're no bother, Mary Elizabeth. You're family!"

Josiah walked in the door, and Bingo and Jet followed him in. "Company? Hey, Ryan, Mary Elizabeth. What's the occasion?" Then he noticed Mary Elizabeth's condition. "Oh. You okay?"

She nodded. "Better now."

Jenna looked at Josiah and said, "She's going to stay here with us tonight."

"Sure, of course. No problem," said Josiah.

Ryan frowned at Mary Elizabeth. "Are you sure you want to do this, Mary Elizabeth? You've put me into a very awkward position. What am I going to tell your father?"

"Don't tell him anything," said Mary Elizabeth.

"Then he'll definitely come into my house and shoot me."

"Just tell him that she's staying with the sheriff and his wife!" said Josiah.

Ryan smiled at his brother-in-law's confidence in his position. "I could do that, but he'll probably want to come here and see her."

"I won't see him!" said Mary Elizabeth, covering her

face, and the tears starting anew. "Don't make me see him! Not tonight!"

Jenna patted her arm. "No, Mary Elizabeth, if you don't want to see him, I will not make you see him. Don't worry."

Ryan sighed. "Now that that's settled, I better get going. It's getting close to dark." He walked over and kissed the top of Mary Elizabeth's head. "Thanks, Jenna, Josiah, for taking care of her for me. I'll stop by tomorrow morning to pick her up—or else I'll stop by tonight with her father."

Josiah straightened up and put out his chest. "He won't be able to see her, but maybe he could hear her voice." Looking at Mary Elizabeth, he asked, "Would that be okay?"

She nodded but didn't say anything. "All right, then it's settled," said Ryan. "I'm leaving. Can Dolly stay here tonight?"

"Sure," said Josiah. "I'll take care of Dolly. Don't worry about it. You have enough to handle with Mr. Mills. Good luck with that!"

Ryan walked out the door, climbed onto Treetop's back, and rode away, all the while wondering what he was going to tell Mr. Mills when he arrived at his house. It was getting dark, but he was almost there. He had decided what he was going to tell him—the truth—or as close to the truth as he could get without divulging any information about the new Red Bluff.

He ground tied Treetop while he knocked on the door of the house. Mr. Mills answered. When he saw Ryan— alone, without Mary Elizabeth—he looked scared. "What's happened to her? Is she hurt? Is she alive? What have you done with my daughter?"

"She's alive, and she's fine. But she's a little hurt—nothing much—just scraped hands and knees."

"Well, where is she, then?" he demanded. "If she's okay, why isn't she with you?"

"She's at the sheriff's house—with my sister, Jenna. She's staying the night there."

"Why would she be there when she has a perfectly good home to come home to?"

Ryan shrugged. "I tried to talk her out of it, believe me. But you know how women are."

At this shred of camaraderie, Mr. Mills showed a slight smile and nodded his head. "Yes, I'm afraid I do." Then he tilted his head and looked at Ryan. "How did it happen? You didn't knock her down, did you?"

"I swear to you, Sir, I had nothing to do with it. I did go to get her after it happened, though." Ryan knew he was opening a door that he really didn't want to open, but it felt right.

Mr. Mills nodded his head again and said, "Oh. So did this maybe happen where you *came from*?"

Ryan looked him straight in the eyes and said, "Yes."

"I don't trust this whole situation! I want to see her! Is she at your house?"

"I'm not lying to you, Mr. Mills. Mary Elizabeth is safe and sound with the sheriff and my sister, Jenna." Reluctantly, he added, "I'll take you there if you want."

"Fine! Let me get my jacket!" Mr. Mills disappeared into the house, slamming the door behind him, and came out a minute later carrying a lantern. He slammed the door again and said, "Let's go." Then he quickly strode into the barn to get his horse.

Ryan followed him into the barn while Mr. Mills brushed and saddled his horse. He walked him out and

239

asked Ryan to hold him while he returned the lantern into the house.

When he came back out of the house, Ryan handed him the reins to his horse. "Mr. Mills, she won't see you. And neither Jenna nor Josiah will make her see you."

"We'll see about that when we get there." He swung up on his horse. "And I want to stop at your house on the way!"

"Fine." Ryan sighed. "It's a good thing there's a full moon tonight. They live out of town."

"I'm sure we'll be fine. Let's go."

Mr. Mills kicked his horse, and it bolted out into the street. Ryan urged Treetop forward and rode beside Mr. Mills. They were in town in no time. Lights shone in some of the windows—upstairs at the doctor's office, in the saloon, at the hotel, at the sheriff's office—and Mr. Mills stopped there and announced, "I'll be right back." He walked into the sheriff's office and came out brushing off his pants and carrying a lantern. "Dang puppy! Got hair all over me." Looking at Ryan, he said, "I trust you don't mind my checking your place?"

"Do what you have to do, Mr. Mills. I told you where she is."

Mr. Mills disappeared into Ryan's dark store, and Nick came out and stood in front of Ryan with the puppy in his arms. "What's this about?"

Ryan leaned down to whisper to Nick. "Mary Elizabeth got her purse stolen in Red Bluff. They knocked her down, and she skinned her hands and knees. She didn't want to face her folks, so she's staying at Jenna and Josiah's tonight. Mills doesn't believe it, so he's checking my house, and then we're riding out to Josiah's."

"At night? Lucky there's a full moon." Nick looked up

into the lantern light moving around upstairs at Ryan's. "Is there anything up there that he shouldn't see?"

Ryan nodded. "Of course there is. Nobody goes upstairs. My iPad is up there, and I have a battery powered lantern, and my solar charger may be in the window. What can I do? I didn't want him to think I was hiding Mary Elizabeth in my house!"

Nick motioned over his shoulder as the light disappeared from upstairs and came closer to the street. "Here he comes. Good luck." He walked back into the sheriff's office as Mr. Mills emerged from Ryan's store.

"She's not in there," he said in passing before he returned the lantern to Nick. When he came out again, he jumped up on his horse. "Let's go."

"Fine, Mr. Mills, but I told you that she wouldn't see you."

"But I could hear her voice, right? If she's really there, I can hear her voice."

Ryan nodded and led the way out of town. "We'll be there soon."

After a few minutes of walking, Mr. Mills said, "Let's canter so we'll get there quicker."

"No! I am not going to canter my horse in the dark to prove to you that I'm telling the truth."

Mr. Mills grumbled but didn't say anything more until he saw the lights at Jenna and Josiah's ranch. "She's in there?"

"Yes, Sir. Safe and sound, like I said."

They rode to the beginning of the driveway, and at that vantage point in the dark, they could see shadows in the windows. In one window was a man and a woman, and in the other window was a woman. "That's her. I recognize her from here. She looks all right. But why

241

wouldn't she want to come home?"

"I think that's a question you should ask yourself, Mr. Mills," said Ryan quietly. Without waiting for a response, he added, "You've seen what you wanted to see. Let's go home."

No one said a word on the way back to town, and Ryan was beginning to feel relieved when Mr. Mills spoke up. "You know, Ryan, there were some powerful strange things that I found upstairs in your house. Maybe we could talk about that sometime."

CHAPTER FIFTY-ONE

EARLY THE FOLLOWING morning, Ryan walked to the livery to brush and saddle Treetop. "Sorry, ole boy, you're not used to so much action, are you? And twice in two days!" The horse nickered, and Ryan scratched his neck in his "itchy-place" that he loved.

When they got halfway to the ranch, Ryan saw Josiah heading into town. "Hey, stranger," he called.

"Hey, Ryan. Mary Elizabeth is feeling much better today. Jenna loaned her a dress, so she wouldn't have to go home in the torn, bloody skirt. Jenna figured there would be fewer questions that way, and Mary Elizabeth agreed. We don't need an irate father snooping around over *there*."

"Yeah, well, I think we have a problem," said Ryan.

Josiah raised his eyebrows. "*We* have a problem?" He smiled at Ryan.

"Yes, *we*. Last night when I told Mr. Mills that his daughter was fine, but she had been hurt and was now at your house, he insisted on going to see her. So we rode out to your place in the moonlight."

"He never came in." Josiah looked confused.

243

Ryan nodded. "I know. He saw her through the window and felt satisfied that she was safe. But before we left town, he insisted on going through my house to make sure I wasn't hiding her there. And he went upstairs with a lantern that he borrowed from Nick."

"That doesn't mean that he saw your stuff."

"Unfortunately, I'm sure of it. He mentioned it before he went home."

"Oh, no," said Josiah.

"Oh, yes. Now what are we going to do? He's going to want to know the whole story. Do we tell him?"

"I don't know how we can."

"I don't know how we can't. He knows. He just doesn't know all the details. I think we have to tell him."

Josiah shook his head. "Oh, this isn't good at all. He's a very prominent citizen in Red Bluff. If he knows, and if he tells others, I honestly couldn't even imagine what the implications might be."

"You're right. It's dangerous. We need to have a meeting—everybody from the new Red Bluff has to attend. Then we'll decide. What do you think?"

"When do you want to have the meeting?"

"How about today? The sooner the better."

"Don't you usually go to town on Sundays to pick up supplies for the week?"

"Some things are more important than other things. And maybe the meeting will go quickly. Can you get people together? I'll go pick up Mary Elizabeth, and we'll meet you in town."

"Bring Jenna, too! If I know Jenna, she'll have something to say about it!" Josiah waved and rode off with his dog Bingo trailing behind him.

Ryan, eager to see Mary Elizabeth, pressed Treetop to

walk faster toward the ranch. When he got there, Dolly was already saddled and tied to the hitching post in front of the house. He knocked on the door, and Mary Elizabeth answered with a smile on her face. He swept her up in his arms and gave her a big hug and a kiss on the mouth.

"You certainly look different than yesterday." Ryan looked her up and down. "You look good," he said warmly.

"Thank you," said Mary Elizabeth.

"We had a little heart-to-heart girl-talk," said Jenna. "For the first thing, I told her about the evils of corsets and that she should at least loosen hers!"

"Would you mind, Ryan?" asked Mary Elizabeth.

"Not at all. If you never wanted to wear one again, that would be fine, too. I love you for you." He looked at her like he couldn't get enough of the sight of her. "What else did you talk about?"

"Jenna told me in detail about what happened—and almost happened—to Sarah. And about how bad things can happen there *or* here."

"I hope she didn't tell you so much that you want to move there again."

"No, Ryan. I'll never again want to move there. I still don't even want to go back. But I feel better about it, now. After we get married, I'd like you to bring me my laptop, iPad, and iPod, though."

Ryan and Jenna laughed. "Not quite a completely nineteenth-century girl!" Ryan squeezed her shoulder. "I love you. But I'm glad that you don't want to move there." He looked at both women. "Oh! Bad news, Mary Elizabeth." Before she could respond, he continued. "Your father searched my place for you last night and discovered some of my twenty-first-century things. He mentioned it to me. So now we're having a meeting in town to discuss if and what we should tell him."

"Tell him nothing!" said Mary Elizabeth.

"I disagree," said Jenna. "He's your father, Mary Elizabeth, and he has a right to know. Everything."

"Well, come with us into town to the meeting, and you can let your feelings be known." Ryan walked toward the front door.

Jenna shook her head. "I just put Milo to sleep. Neither he nor I are going anywhere. You've heard what I think. I vote to tell him everything. That's all you need. You don't need me."

"Okay, Jenna, I'll tell them what you said. Mary Elizabeth? You ready?"

She smiled up at him. "Ready." She knelt down to pet the dog at her feet. "Good-bye, Jet. It was good to get to know you better." Jet licked her face.

Ryan helped her up on Dolly, then he climbed onto Treetop. "Let's go, my dear! Homeward bound!" He smiled at her.

As they rode away from Jenna's ranch, Mary Elizabeth touched his sleeve and looked at him. "Ryan?"

"Yes, dear?"

"Um, I don't know how to say this without just saying it. Do you still want to marry me?"

He pulled back the reins on Treetop and looked at her. "Yes, of course I do! Nothing has changed. Why would you think that?"

She looked down, not able to meet his face. "Because I googled myself on the internet and found out that I'd written and published a bunch of books."

"That's great, Mary Elizabeth! I'm so proud of you! I

knew you were a writer!" Then he reached out and tilted her head back so he could look into her eyes. "What does that have to do with me not wanting to marry you?"

"The books were all published under Mary Elizabeth Mills."

"Is that all? It's probably a pen name! No big deal, Mary Elizabeth. We'll get married whenever you want to." Ryan hoped it would be soon, so he added, "As soon as you want to."

"Really, Ryan, do you mean that?"

"Yes, of course I do!"

"How about tomorrow?"

"Tomorrow! I don't know if we could manage to get married *tomorrow*. But if you really want to, I'll try my best to arrange it."

CHAPTER FIFTY-TWO

WHEN THEY ARRIVED in town, Ryan said, "Where do you think the meeting is?"

Mary Elizabeth looked around. "Look! There's a note on Josiah's door!" She moved Dolly closer to the door so she could read it. "It says, 'If you need the sheriff, he is at the hotel.' But wouldn't Nick be there to fill in for him?"

Ryan shook his head. "Nick is from *there*, also. He would be at the meeting. Let's ride over there." They rode the short distance down the street, got off their horses, and tied them in front of the hotel. "Let's go in."

Ryan opened the door and let Mary Elizabeth walk in first. Several tables in the restaurant had been pushed together to accommodate all the people, who were all talking among themselves. They sat down at two seats that had been saved for them. Another empty seat beside Josiah was for Jenna.

"Where's Jenna?" Josiah leaned across the table to Ryan.

"She said she had just put the baby down, and she wasn't coming, but she thought he should be told *every-*

248

thing."

"Okay, then." Louder, Josiah addressed the group, "Let's call the meeting to order. Everybody knows what we're here for, right? Mr. Mills, the bank president, has accidentally discovered some twenty-first-century items at Ryan's."

"I told you bringing those fancy electronic gadgets here would get you in trouble, Grandson!" said Granny.

Ryan shrugged. "I never expected anybody upstairs who I didn't invite. But he thought I had Mary Elizabeth hiding there."

"It doesn't really matter how it happened. It just happened, and there's nothing we can do about that now. The question is, do we tell John Mills the truth or do we try to come up with a good lie to appease him?" Josiah looked out at the faces.

"Why wouldn't we want to tell him the truth?" asked Sarah.

"John Mills is a prominent citizen in Red Bluff. I'm not sure how he would respond to the truth. Would he tell everyone? Would he want to close down the passage? If he wanted to, he could easily get the whole town behind him to do anything that he wanted." Josiah glanced at all the people at the table.

Doc, Kat's husband, spoke up. "*I* am also a prominent citizen of Red Bluff. And honestly, I don't think that has anything to do with anything. Everybody has friends and could get them to go their way. Mary Elizabeth, what do you think? He's *your* father."

"I don't know. The whole thing is my fault, and I apologize to everyone for making a mess of things." She put her head down and leaned it against Ryan's shoulder.

He put his arm around her and said, "What happened

249

to you was *not* your fault. It's just an unfortunate set of circumstances that might have gotten us into trouble, that's all. No one's fault."

Granny stood up. "Frankly, I don't see what all the fuss is about. Just tell the man the truth. Just because he can be a jerk, doesn't mean that he would do something to hurt his only daughter. At least not deliberately."

"But if he insisted on closing down the passage, it would hurt some of us a great deal, but would hurt Mary Elizabeth very little," Matthew, Sarah's husband, said.

"Really, what are the chances that is what he'd want to do? And for what reason? It doesn't make any sense," said Rachel.

Granny stood up again. "I find this whole conversation ridiculous. Let's vote on it and see where we're at."

Josiah raised his voice. "You heard her. Granny thinks that we should just vote on it. Does anybody think that it would be more valuable to discuss it any more?"

"It's all conjecture," said Nick. "Nobody really has any idea what Mr. Mills might do with the information. Do you have any idea, Mary Elizabeth?"

She shook her head but didn't speak. When she thought about it, she agreed with Nick. Even *she*, his own daughter, had no idea what he might do with information like that. Would he do anything to hurt anyone? She doubted it. More likely that he would use the information to make money. *That* would be something that her father would do. "I think the only bad thing that my father might do is to try to make money with the information."

Ryan laughed. "Didn't Zack give everyone in town a list of valuable coins? *All* of us are trying to do that! I agree with Granny, let's vote."

Josiah stood up. "My wife, Jenna, told Ryan that she votes to tell Mr. Mills everything. Since I have a sense of the way this is going, I'm asking it backwards. So, who is opposed to telling Mr. Mills about the future?"

Mary Elizabeth spoke up, "I thought I was, but after hearing everyone and after thinking about it, I'm not opposed anymore."

"Anyone else? Opposed?" No one raised their hand. "Okay, who is in favor of telling Mr. Mills everything?" Everyone raised their hands. "It's settled then. We'll tell him. Okay, who is going to go get him and tell him? Mary Elizabeth?"

"I'm surprised he's not here already. He expected me home earlier than this."

And then the door to the hotel swung open, and Mr. Mill strolled into the room. Ignoring all the people, he looked at Mary Elizabeth and said, "I thought you were coming straight home after your little jaunt yesterday and last night!" It wasn't a question.

Before Mary Elizabeth could respond, Ryan spoke up. "Mr. Mills. Mary Elizabeth did not go straight home because we asked her to attend this meeting. And this meeting was set up because of what you found upstairs at my house."

"I'm listening."

"Maybe you should sit down, Mr. Mills," said Josiah, as he patted the seat next to him.

After Mr. Mills sat down, Josiah looked at Ryan. "Somebody who's from there should tell him. Ryan?"

"Wait!" said Rachel. "I know we all agreed, but shouldn't we get him to swear or something?"

"Young lady," said Mr. Mills, "I *never* swear!"

"I'm having second thoughts," said Matthew. "What if

251

he tells somebody?"

Ryan frowned, tilted his head, and looked at Mr. Mills. "Can you keep a secret?"

"A secret! Of course I can keep a secret! I'm a Mason!" He held up his ring to prove it.

Nick stood up and held out his ring. "I'm a Mason, too!"

"Okay, Mr. Mills. We'll give it to you straight. We—all the newcomers in town that you see here, plus my sister, Jenna—are all from the future."

Mr. Mills' stoic face did not change. "I would normally laugh in your faces, except the objects I saw in your house yesterday, Ryan, were not normal objects. Tell me more."

"Jenna got stuck in a snowstorm and accidentally discovered the cave. Then she moved here, I moved here —well, we all moved here."

"If those objects are any indication, the future must be filled with all kinds of miraculous things. Why would you want to move back *here*?"

"Because we like it here better," said Nick.

"And some of us fell in love and didn't have any choice," said Kat, snuggling up to Doc.

"Well, how far into the future are we talking?"

"More than a hundred years in the future," said Ryan. "1871 here, 2015 there."

Mr. Mills' eyes widened in shock. "Okay, say I believe you, and I think I have to. The question is—when can I go see this place for myself?"

The table erupted with talking and laughter. "We never expected that!" said Granny.

"But we should have," said Josiah.

"How *soon* do you want to see it? I still have to make a

run there today to pick up supplies for the store," said Ryan.

"Today is soon enough for me! I'll go home now and get Cora." Mr. Mills stood up.

"Do you think Mama will want to go?" asked Mary Elizabeth.

"She's going," he said. "And you?"

"No," said Mary Elizabeth. "After what happened, I'm never going back."

"What did happen there?" asked Mr. Mills.

"Someone knocked her down and stole her purse," said Ryan. And then Mary Elizabeth held up her hands to show him the scraped areas.

Mr. Mills pointed to her. "You are going. You don't think something like that—or worse—could happen here? Look at what happened with Sarah. That could have been disastrous. No, Mary Elizabeth. You will not go home and hide your head in the sand. *You* are going with us today, young lady!"

Before Mary Elizabeth could say a word, Ryan said, "I agree with him, Mary Elizabeth. You'll be safe with all of us."

"Okay," she said reluctantly.

"I'm going to get Cora. Where should I meet you?"

"Wait, Mr. Mills. You can't bring your wagon there. I'll come pick you up," said Ryan.

"We can't all fit in your wagon. There are only two seats. Mary Elizabeth, how about you drive over there with your mother. And Ryan and I can ride our horses."

Mary Elizabeth stood up. "I have a better idea. I don't know the trail that well. How about Ryan drives Mama, and you and I ride? I have my own horse now."

CHAPTER FIFTY-THREE

WHEN THEY EMERGED from the cave, Ryan driving her mother in the wagon, and she and her father riding behind, Mary Elizabeth couldn't have been happier. Her father had already complimented her on her new horse, Blue, and how well she rode. Of course, since she had ridden his horse a week earlier, he couldn't exactly say that she was a lousy rider! But here they were, riding along together, talking—really talking—and her mother and Ryan in the wagon talking and laughing together. After they went through the cave, and when the wagon bumped down the makeshift trail to meet the main trail, Mary Elizabeth and her father rode around the wagon so they were in front.

"You want to race?" Mary Elizabeth raised her eyebrows at her father in a challenge.

"Oh, no. Rojo would run your new horse into the ground. I don't want to embarrass you in front of Ryan."

"Don't be so sure that you're going to win, Papa. Blue is fast. He's a thoroughbred."

Her father shrugged. "I doubt it, Mary Elizabeth. That horse can't beat Rojo. No horse can."

"Want to bet?" She turned around to Ryan and her mother. "Mama? Say one, two, three, go. Okay?"

"Okay, dear," her mother called out. "One! Two! Three! Go!"

And without waiting to see if her father had taken off or not, Mary Elizabeth and Blue ran down the trail. She leaned low over Blue's neck. Thinking she heard hoof beats, she turned quickly to see her father gaining on her. When she encouraged Blue to run faster, he ran like the wind, leaving her father behind. Before she knew it, the gate had come into view, so she gently pulled Blue up into a stop. Her father and Rojo stopped behind her.

"I can't believe you beat me." Her father patted Rojo's neck. "He must be off his feed or something."

"Don't make excuses, Papa, just congratulate me on beating you."

"No, I really think that Rojo—you're right, Mary Elizabeth. Congratulations."

After a few minutes, Ryan, her mother, and the wagon pulled up behind them, so Mary Elizabeth opened the gate and rode ahead to the next one, while her father closed the gate behind the wagon. A few minutes later, they were all at the barn. The horses were put up and watered, and the four people approached the house.

"Good. Zack and Madison are home," said Ryan, pointing to their cars. "I'd like them to meet you."

"What are those things?"

"Those are cars, Papa. That's how people get around in the future. They only ride horses for pleasure."

Her father shook his head. "Amazing!"

When Zack opened the door and looked at them in surprise, Ryan made all the introductions, and everyone settled into the living room. Zack explained the television, stereo, and the laptop that was on the coffee table.

"I have one, too!" Mary Elizabeth said, disappearing into the bedroom, and returning with her own laptop. "This one is mine, and this," she held up the iPod, "and this!" She held up the iPad.

"But what's a laptop good for?" asked her father.

"Zack, show him a spreadsheet," Ryan said. "He'll be able to appreciate that."

When Zack showed him how the columns added up by themselves, her father was thoroughly impressed. "But these things must have cost money, and in a hundred years, everything must have gotten more expensive. How could you afford all this? Did you buy them for her, Ryan?"

Ryan shook his head. "Zack, do you have your coin book to show Mr. Mills?"

"I bought one! I'll go get mine!" Mary Elizabeth took the laptop, iPod, and iPad back to the bedroom and returned with the new coin book that she had bought on the day she got hurt. "Here, Papa. Take a look."

With each page he turned, the oohs and aahs got louder. "A quarter from *our* time is worth this much money in *this* time? Unbelievable! Is that what you were doing at the bank, Mary Elizabeth? Picking out some of these coins?"

She nodded. "I made more than twenty thousand dollars." Looking at him in a mock arrogant way, she said, "*I* can buy *you* a laptop if you want!"

"Remember Granny's birthday party a year ago? There were some desserts there——"

"You want some ice cream, Mr. Mills?" Zack raised his eyebrows. "I can take you in a ride in the car and bring back some ice cream. Are you interested?"

He sprang up and said, "Sure am! Let's go! Cora, would you like to go with us?"

"No thank you, dear. I'd rather stay here with Mary Elizabeth."

After Zack and Mr. Mills left, Madison said, "Cora, would you like to see the new inventions in the kitchen? I think you'll be pleasantly surprised." Cora followed Madison into the kitchen, and Mary Elizabeth sat down on the sofa next to Ryan.

"Can you believe this?"

He put his arm around her. "No, I can't. Who would have thought that your father would come to the twenty-first century and be so open to everything that it has to offer. Even ice cream!"

Ryan looked at her. "You haven't had any ice cream! I've never even taken you out to dinner here. I'm sorry!"

"It's okay, Ryan. You took me other places." She looked into his eyes. "Besides, we still have time."

"Your father forced you to come today. So you'll come back with just me sometime?"

She nodded and put her head on his shoulder. Then her mother and Madison walked by.

"I'm showing her the bathroom, Mary Elizabeth."

"Oh, no, if you do that, she'll be wanting one of those necessaries like Jenna has!" Then she looked at Ryan. "Can *we* have one of those necessaries like Jenna has?"

"I'm ahead of you. I already had it on my list to buy lumber for it today. And lumber for a corral as well. I figured you'd want that big blue horse of yours close."

"Ezra told you!"

Ryan looked confused. "No, I just know you!" He kissed her gently on the lips.

By the time Zack and her father returned, Mary Elizabeth, her mother, Ryan, and Madison had been sitting on the sofa talking and laughing like they had known each other for years. Zack had not only bought ice cream, but he had brought home a huge meal called a pizza that was delicious. And with ice cream for dessert, everyone came away from the table happy.

When they went back to the living room, Mr. Mills looked at Ryan. "Okay, Ryan, this is all fine, and now I know where you're from. But the question is, when are you going to marry my daughter?"

Mary Elizabeth said, "Papa, I'd like to get married tomorrow, but Ryan wasn't sure he could arrange it."

"I'm going to try, though, Sir," said Ryan.

"No need, Ryan. I will send a telegram as soon as we return, and I'll have someone there tomorrow to marry you. Guaranteed! That's the least I can do." Then he glanced at Ryan. "If that's okay with you, that is."

"Yes, Mr. Mills, that's fine. She is your daughter, after all."

"Madison? Zack? Any chance you can come to our wedding tomorrow afternoon?"

Zack put his arm around Madison. "We wouldn't miss it, Mary Elizabeth!"

When her parents were deep in discussion with Zack and Madison, Mary Elizabeth looked at Ryan. "I love you so much, Ryan. And I'm going to love being your wife. What do you think about me using a pen name of Mary Elizabeth Mills for my writing?"

Ryan's eyes crinkled with delight, and then he hugged her. "I love you, too, Mary Elizabeth *Leyton*."

THE END